FLIRTING
WITH *Forever*

New York Times & USA Today Bestselling Author
KENDALL RYAN

D0920729

Flirting with Forever
Copyright © 2018 Kendall Ryan

Content Editing by
Elaine York

Copy Editing by
Pam Berehulke

Cover Design and Formating by
Uplifting Designs

About the Book

I've waited years for the perfect girl, yet she was right in front of me all along.

My best friend, Natalie, has been by my side through everything. Leaning on my shoulder, borrowing my sweatshirts…and making my pants too tight when she flashes me that sassy smile that drives me crazy.

But she has no idea about that last part. She doesn't have a clue I've felt this way about her for years.

Until one night after too many cocktails, we fall into bed together.

I'm flirting with my forever…she just doesn't know it yet.

This book is a sexy, slow-burning best-friends-to-lovers romance with a guaranteed HEA and no cheating. Dive in, and get ready to melt for Cam!

CHAPTER
One

Camden

"A beer for this guy." I motion to the bartender to bring another for my miserable-looking buddy. Jack and I have been friends for fifteen years, and I've never seen him this torn up over a girl. *Ever.* Heartbreak isn't a good look on a man. That's an undeniable truth.

A bottle of beer appears a few moments later, and I push it closer to him. "Drink up."

"Thanks, man," Jack says, taking a long swig.

It isn't often that I volunteer to be the designated driver, but when I got the call from Jack this afternoon that his long-term girlfriend broke up with him over text, I knew he'd be drinking a bit heavier than our usual one or two reserved for

Friday nights. We can't drink the way we used to in college without calling most of Saturday a complete wash.

But tonight is different. He deserves to work out his problems with his drink of choice without worrying about getting home to our apartment safely, so I told him I'd stick to water for the evening.

"All I'm saying is she could have had the decency to say it to my face," Jack says, wiping the beer foam off his lips with the side of his hand. "What kind of person ends a year-long relationship over text message?"

"The kind of person who doesn't deserve you," I say, gesturing to the bartender for another cold one. He pops the top off a bottle for Jack and slides over a bowl of bar mix for me.

Jack sighs, sliding his empty beer bottle to the bartender. "Yeah, I guess you're right." He groans, staring down the neck of his beer like the answer to his relationship problems is floating in there somewhere.

"Damn straight I'm right. Name one time I've been wrong in all the years we've been friends."

He rests his chin on his fist but doesn't answer. Either because he can't think of a time, or because the alcohol has made his brain fuzzy, or maybe because he's fallen into a beer-induced sleep. I look over at him to see if he's still upright. Thank God, he is. I don't want to have to carry him out of this bar.

My phone buzzes twice in my pocket—it's Natalie, checking in to make sure I'm getting Jack good and drunk. Given the circumstances, I figured it was best that it was a "no girls allowed" kind of evening, but it's been a long time since he and I have been out without Natalie. I can't blame her for feeling a little left out.

When I glance over, I notice Jack is messing around on his phone for what has to be the tenth time tonight. Odds are good that he's already hitting up some other girl. I love Jack to death, but he's always been a bit of a player. I'm actually a little surprised his most recent relationship lasted this long.

"Natalie was checking in to make sure you were getting adequately hammered," I say, holding up my phone to snap a picture of Jack and his collection of empty bottles. He sets his phone down and poses mid-chug, giving the camera an enthusiastic thumbs-up. I send the photo to Natalie as evidence that I'm doing my job.

"Man, I'm so damn lucky to have you two," Jack says between long sips. "What would I do without you guys?"

A little bit of alcohol always brings out his sentimental side, but I'm game for a stroll down memory lane. I decide I'll play along.

"I hardly remember life before the three of us were friends," I admit, shoving my phone back in my pocket. "My brain must have just erased every memory prior to sophomore-year biology class."

"The three amigos!" Jack hollers, raising his beer in a toast. "The best lab group ever!"

"Yeah, only because I carried all of our grades by doing all the work," I tease, clinking my water glass against his beer.

"Hey, it's not Natalie's fault that she was so bad at biology, and that I had such a hair-trigger gag reflex looking at pig eyeballs," he argues with a sloppy finger wag.

Four must be the magic number of beers for

Jack. I've got to remember to give him grief tomorrow about what a lightweight he's become.

"Yeah, I remember. That private school she transferred in from didn't teach bio until junior year. What was your excuse?" I pick through the bar mix and flick a peanut at Jack's head.

"Laziness and a queasy stomach, mostly," he says after trying to bat the peanut away a little too late. It hits him square between the eyes and bounces across the floor. His reflexes are gone; he's officially drunk. "You should be thanking me. That was the class that made you want to become a doctor. I was just letting you discover your passion."

I'm a pediatrician, and he's right, I love my job, so I really can't argue. "And I was just saving you from flunking science class."

Downing the rest of his beer, he shoots me the bird and then reaches for the bar mix to find some ammo of his own, eventually settling on a pretzel rod. I let him take his shot, lining up the pretzel like a javelin and tossing it at me. He's obviously aiming for the "third" me that he sees and he misses by a long shot. The pretzel goes hurtling across the bar, nailing some unsuspecting sucker in the back of the head.

"And that's our cue to close the tab." I wave over the bartender and slide my AmEx card across the bar, which gets me a confused look from Jack.

"Why the hell are you paying?" he asks, his brow furrowed. "You just got water."

"Yeah, and you just got dumped," I say, scribbling my signature across the receipt and stuffing a ten-dollar bill in the tip jar. "Now, come on. Let's get out of here."

As I walk and Jack stumbles across the parking lot, I shoot Natalie a quick text to let her know I've completed my mission of getting Jack drunk and that we're headed home. The radio starts as soon as I turn the key in the ignition—some catchy pop love song that Jack immediately switches. He stays diligent on the radio dial, changing the station every time a song mentions a girl or a kiss, or anything else even sort of related to romance.

I feel bad for the poor guy. Apparently, his ex has left his heart in freaking tatters, and this is so out of my element with him. He's always been the love 'em and leave 'em heartbreaker, not at all the type to get dumped and feel like shit about it.

"All these goddamn love songs," he mumbles, throwing in the towel and shutting the radio off altogether. "I'm sick of this shit. Women suck. All they do is steal your sweatshirts, cram all their shit into your bathroom, and then leave when they're bored of you."

Before I can form a counterargument, he's pointing at a fast-food restaurant ahead. "Dude, let's get something to eat."

I don't even bother trying to stifle my annoyance as I pull up to the drive-through, asking the girl on the intercom to give us a minute to decide.

"What do you want, Jack? A burger? Fries?"

"I want a woman who isn't gonna completely screw me over," he grumbles, giving the glove compartment a swift kick of frustration.

"Burger and fries, it is."

I place his order and pull forward to pay. Jack is either too buzzed or too sad to give me shit about paying this time, but his mood lightens a bit when I pass him the bag of hot, greasy goodness packed with more calories than he's probably consumed all day—well, except for the liquid kind of calories. Hopefully, those fries will soak up some of the alcohol in his system and make his hungover ass slightly more bearable tomorrow.

He tears into his fries with a satisfied grunt. "Fries are so good. Why would I ever even need a woman when I have fries?"

"I'm going to go out on a limb here and say that it's probably because fries can't get you off. Although, I will admit that I've eaten a steak a time or two that almost gave me a happy ending." I pull into a parking spot nearby and settle back into my seat.

"I think I've gotta go on a hiatus, dude," he says around another mouthful. "Swear off women for a while. Get my head straight."

My gaze swings over to his in stunned fascination. "That's cute. But there's no way in hell you'd last more than a week. Two, tops."

As long as Jack and I have been friends, he's always had a girl in the picture. Whether it's a girlfriend, a hookup buddy, or just somebody he met on a dating app, there have been very few nights in our apartment where Jack hasn't been sharing his bed with someone. Swearing off girls will be harder for him than swearing off beer—or fries. And that's saying something.

"Bullshit. You really think I'm that weak?"

He seems genuinely insulted, so I try a gentler approach. "Come on, man. You've been getting it on the regular for as long as I can remember. There's no way you can go without."

"I've got a perfectly good hand. I'll be fine . . . women are the root of all my evils. I'm in need of an exorcism," he says into the greasy paper bag, digging out his burger. "No more women. I'm announcing it now. Hold me to it." He points at me with a fry.

Resisting the urge to roll my eyes, I reach for a couple of fries. "I'll remind you of that when you meet some blonde at the gym next week and want to bring her home. You'll fold in a heartbeat."

"Like hell I will. How much do you want to bet I can make it a whole month without hooking up with anyone?"

Is he seriously going to make a wager on this? I'm not much of a gambler, but this sounds like a bet I'll be guaranteed to win, so why the hell not?

"All right, how about this?" I turn in my seat to look him straight in the eye so he knows I mean business. "I'll do it with you. No women, no sex, no hookups. I bet I can hold out way longer than you. Easy."

Jack rolls his eyes. "Oh, sure, easy for you. You're practically a monk."

It's been a long couple of months' worth of his jokes insisting that I must be a born-again virgin with how little action I've been getting. Yeah, maybe I am in the midst of a dry spell, but it's no big deal. And working long shifts in the pediatric wing of the hospital downtown certainly isn't helping. But I'll take whatever he's gonna bet me, because I know what a dry spell feels like. My homeboy here has no freaking idea what he's in for. This win will be like taking candy from a baby.

"Listen, are you for real about this bet or not?"

Jack weighs it over with a few more fries, presumably trying to decide if his hand can really cut it. "You know what? Let's do it," he says, pumping his fist in the air and sending fries flying throughout my car.

I love my job. I really do. Not to say that I

wouldn't mind getting laid in the near future. I've had a few potential prospects catch my eye, but if we're betting on it, what's another month of beating it in the shower?

"And whoever breaks first . . ." I chew one fry slowly, partially to build the suspense, partially to buy myself time to think of what we're betting on. A round of drinks? Cleaning the apartment for a month? No, this is some serious shit. The stakes are high. We need to make this deal worth keeping it in our pants for.

"Whoever caves first has to do the other's laundry for the rest of the year."

A sinister grin creeps across Jack's face. "Done." He wipes the fry grease from his hands onto a napkin before slapping his hand into mine.

"It's a deal then," I say with a firm handshake and a confident smirk. "So you might want to say good-bye to that hookup from last year who I've been watching you text all night. Because that's sure as hell not happening anytime soon."

My own phone chirps from the cupholder and I grab it. "It's Nat again," I say to Jack, opening the text.

> Now we're all single. Lonely
> Hearts Club unite.

I stare down at her message and frown. As far as I know, Natalie is single by choice. This is the first time I've heard her say she's lonely, and something inside me doesn't like it.

> Surely you're not lacking for
> offers, Miss Moore.

She is a Moore, whether she likes it or not—a trust-fund baby whose father's wealth is reported by the media much more often than she would like.

> Oh, hush, you can't comment on
> that.

Smiling, I can practically hear the sarcasm in Natalie's text.

> And why not?

> Because you're a twenty-nine-

```
year-old doctor, for starters.
Women line up to drop their
panties for you.
```

I chuckle and shove another fry into my mouth.

```
Not interested in a gold digger.
```

```
Same. But if you know of any
good guys out there, send them
my way.
```

A weird tingle creeps down my spine. There are only two good guys I can vouch for, and both are inside this vehicle. Jack may be a player, but he's honest and loyal to the women he dates and hooks up with. They know the deal, and are okay with the mutually beneficial arrangement. Him being heartbroken over getting dumped is new for him and says volumes about his maturity level. Me, on the other hand, I'm not entirely sure why Natalie's words affect me the way they do, and I chalk it up to being around the heartbroken drunkard sitting next to me.

"What's that look for?" Jack asks, his burger halfway to his mouth.

"Hmm? Oh, nothing." I set my phone back into the cupholder. "Just texting with Natalie."

"Good. Because now that you've taken this vow with me, Nat better be the only female you're texting with these days."

"Noted."

Why does the prospect of that not bother me in the slightest?

CHAPTER Two

Natalie

Knockity-knock-knock.

"Special delivery."

I poke my head through the bathroom doorway and call, "Coming!" Sound travels easily in my condo, so I have no worries that Cam didn't hear me.

Moments later, I open the front door. It's Cam, holding up a small pink box with a promising doughnut sticker on the side. As I tackle him with a hug, he saves said treats from being crushed by my enthusiasm. Before I release him, I breathe in his masculine, fresh scent. It's comforting, familiar, like a warm cup of chamomile tea or a new spool of yarn.

We part and he takes a step back, his gaze lowering as he appraises me with a frown. "You're wearing a towel," he says, still holding the doughnut box above my head. *Oops.*

"Well, yeah, I was about to shower," I respond defensively.

Swiping the box from his hands, I head straight for my kitchen. I haven't eaten all morning, so I'm more than ready to dig into this pastry, regardless of whether I'm properly clothed.

"What'd you get me?" I ask, spinning the box around on my kitchen counter, eager to open it.

"Something new," he says, leaning against the countertop.

"New?" I peel open the box. Inside sit a dozen decadent doughnuts. I select a chocolate-vanilla-swirl doughnut with frosting drizzled on top and take a nibble. A groan escapes me as the frosting melts devilishly on my tongue.

"You, sir, are bad for my waistline," I say, scolding him through a mouthful of sugary goodness.

"Stop. Your waistline is perfect."

I feel my cheeks grow ever-so-slightly warm. "Not according to the personal trainer I pay a small fortune to each month," I mumble around a mouthful of pastry. "I'm going to hop in the shower, but feel free to hang out."

"Sounds good."

I step into the shower, enjoying the way the hot water relaxes my aching muscles.

"Got plans for tonight?" Cam asks.

Through the sheer curtain, I can pick out his tall frame in the bathroom mirror. He's leaning against the door frame, politely facing away. For a doctor who surely sees all sorts of bodies all day, *every* day, Cam is very aware of his presence in the living space of a naked friend. *It's cute.*

"Plans? Sort of. Jack set me up with a guy from work, actually." Excited, I find myself smiling. I haven't been on a date in eons. I can almost hear Jack's voice clearly in my head, correcting my assumptions about tonight's meet-up.

"Don't jump to conclusions. It's not a date," he would say. "You're just meeting one of my friendlier bartenders for a drink. Very casual."

Apparently, I'm pretty damn lonely if I'm allowing Jack to set me up with one of his employees. *What if we have nothing to talk about? What if he's a total waste of space and I'm left struggling to carry the conversation? I hate carrying the conversation.* As I lather shampoo into my hair, an idea occurs to me. "Do you want to come hang out at the bar with me tonight?"

There's a long pause. I wait and finish rinsing my hair.

"Sure."

I turn off the water and peek out of the shower. Cam turns to meet my gaze, the only thing between his eyes and my naked body a flimsy curtain. I give him my prettiest smile. "Want to help me pick out an outfit too?"

"Okay." His voice is gruff, and his gaze darts from mine to the worn wooden floor.

Moments later, we're in my room, me perusing my closet in my underwear, and Cam sitting at the foot of my bed, staring down at the floor, being useless.

"Sexy underwear definitely isn't necessary," I

mutter, thinking aloud. "It's not like he's going to see any of that on the first date."

"What qualifies as sexy underwear?" he asks. I look back at him with my eyebrows raised. Interestingly, there's no humor in his expression. He seems legitimately curious.

"Well . . ." I pause, considering my next words. "Sexy usually means lace or silk."

"So those aren't?" he asks, gesturing to my own dull, uninteresting ensemble.

"These are cotton!" I laugh. "I got them from the supermarket. Oh, Cam. Have you ever seen a woman in her sexy underwear?" Teasing him is almost too easy, though it's usually split between Jack and myself. And since Jack is busy at work, I guess I'll have to pick up the slack.

"I consider all underwear sexy."

We're two single people, alone in a bedroom, talking about lingerie. Shouldn't this be weird? I brush the unfamiliar thought away. Cam is my closest friend. Talking to him about this stuff is . . . well, natural. *Isn't it?*

"Regardless," I say, "I think a guy should put in

a little effort before he gets any of this." I gesture vaguely around my body's private parts. Assuming the conversation is over, I turn back to my closet, rifling through the endless array of colors and fabrics. Why is it always so hard to find something to wear that is both casual *and* subtly sexy?

"Good," he says. "I agree completely."

The only sound is the scrape of hangers in my closet as I eliminate certain options. I can feel Cam's body heat behind me, and I turn, surprised to see he's joined me inside my walk-in closet.

I face him, suddenly aware that I'm standing almost naked in front of him.

His gaze drops from mine, moving over the swell of my modest cleavage to the boy shorts stretched across my hips. "Trust me, speaking strictly from a guy's point of view, these do look sexy on you."

My brain short-circuits. Did Cam just call me sexy?

No, he said my underwear are something a guy would find sexy. Even though they're cotton.

"Good to know," I manage to say, my voice

coming out a little higher than I intended. I clear my throat.

His large hand reaches out and he selects a couple of hangers. "Here. Wear this."

I accept the outfit and turn to put it on while he makes his way back to my bed.

"So, when do you deem it appropriate to put out? Are you a third-date kind of girl, or what?"

"Cam!" I gasp. I can't help the smirk that tugs on my lips as I turn to face him.

"I'm curious." He smiles, and his chiseled features hold a look of amusement and mischief. Or maybe it's just simple fascination. This is a topic we've never covered before in all our years of friendship.

"Definitely not the first date," I state matter-of-factly. "Maybe the second?"

"Really?" His voice is not at all judgmental. Only impressed.

"What? It's been a long time. Do you know how long it's been since I've even been fingered?"

He laughs incredulously and shakes his head.

Maybe our lack of boundaries is peculiar, but to me, it's the mark of an unbreakable friendship.

"I'm not sure I want to know every last detail," he says. "Let's leave some of the mystery alive in our friendship, okay?" I'm still smiling at the ease of this encounter as he continues speaking. "Although, I do appreciate when a woman makes me work for it," he says, his mouth still curled up in amusement.

I smile, thinking about Cam working to win over a girl he likes. He's been single for so long, I'm sure it would do him good to settle down with someone. But whenever I bring up the topic, he steers the conversation elsewhere and falls back on the same old excuses of *never enough time* or *I work too much*, or the infamous cliché of *I'm married to my job*. Eventually, he has to find someone to fall in love with, doesn't he?

• • •

A half hour later, we're sitting at a high-top table at Jack's bar, Easy Goings. I'm wearing dark skinny jeans with a V-neck top and a leather jacket that Cam helped me pick out. Although he approved of nearly every outfit I modeled, we agreed that this was the best "casual pub meet-up" look.

"Do you want to get some appetizers?" I ask him, flipping through the menu. Although I look at the options, I already know I'll order the same thing I always do—fried pickles. I look up, waiting for Cam's response. "Cam?"

"What?" He seems to be assessing something behind the bar. His pretty brown eyes are narrowed in concentration.

"What on earth are you looking at?" I ask him as I follow his gaze to the mirror behind the bar.

Oh. He's been looking at my reflection.

"Order whatever you want," he says, glancing away from where our gazes meet in the mirror. "You know I'll eat just about anything."

"God, I'm actually nervous. Which is weird, right? But what if we have nothing in common?"

"Then he's not worth your time." Cam runs his thumb comfortingly across my knuckles. "Don't worry about it."

"Thank you," I whisper, squeezing his hand. One of the bartenders delivers our drinks, and Cam places an order for fried pickles. I didn't even have to tell him what to order; he just knows me that well.

"So, tell me about the qualities you're looking for in a guy." Cam grins at me. Our love lives aren't normally a topic we cover in such detail, but I like that he cares enough to ask.

I think it over for a moment before responding. "Someone loyal. Kind. And funny. Definitely funny. Gotta make me laugh. So, what's your type?" I ask, returning the question.

"Confident," he says with zero hesitation. "Not too easily stressed by the small stuff. Comfortable with herself and her path in life."

My eyes widen.

"What?" he asks, no doubt bracing himself to be teased.

"I just . . . That was very specific."

He smiles, humming thoughtfully to himself. Even he seemed surprised by his own answer. "I guess it was specific. Someone who can eat her body weight in doughnuts is also a huge plus."

I chuckle and roll my eyes. "Jackass."

Our order is delivered, and I waste no time digging in.

Cam reaches out to tuck a lock of hair behind my ear. "But I also know whoever she is, she'll have to get your seal of approval." He smiles, leaning his chin against his hand. He looks so lovable when he's all relaxed like that. Suddenly, I'm overcome with the desire to show my affection to this man, so I do the only thing I can think of, considering what I have to work with in my arsenal of affection. I push my plate of half-devoured pickles toward him.

"You can have the rest. You've barely touched them." To that, he just smiles at me, flashing his sweetest smile. "Come on," I say. "I feel like you're only pretending to like them, so I don't feel weird ordering a plate."

"Hey, jackasses, don't get too comfortable. Ben just got here." Jack pulls over a nearby stool and hops up on it. "What's going on?" he asks, grinning at us.

"I'm a little nervous that—"

Jack cuts me off with a hand in front of my face. He gestures to the appetizer plate between us and looks at Cam, his eyes wide, and shakes his head dramatically. "Dude. You let her eat fried pickles? Tonight of all nights?" He then drops his voice. "You know they make her gassy." Cam snickers into his beer, not disagreeing with him.

"You know I can hear you," I mutter, annoyed at how well my best friends know me.

As Cam attempts to contain his laughter, the familiar sound reminds me that I can never be mad at these goons for more than a second.

"I'm heading to the bathroom," I say, swatting Jack's hand away.

"Don't fly away!" Jack calls after me. *Another fart joke. Fantastic.*

"I'm freshening up, you jerks!" I hold up my lipstick tube like a classy middle finger.

"That's awesome, but I stock canned air freshener in the ladies' room just for you, Nat. You may want to use it as body spray or some shit while you're at it." Walking away, all I hear is the laughter of the two Neanderthals behind me. God, I both hate and love those twits.

In the ladies' room, I take in my reflection in the mirror, following the soft lines of each curve peeking out of the jacket Cam helped me select. He was right. I smile, all dimples and rosy cheeks. He's never steered me wrong. I do look good to-night.

With a touch more lipstick and maybe another cocktail, I can get through this date.

Here's hoping.

CHAPTER Three

Camden

"Are you Natalie?" A guy with a scruffy five o'clock shadow and trendy black jeans stops beside Natalie's bar stool. In four seconds, I've sized him up, and I can already tell this guy won't be good enough for her.

Her face lights up in a smile. "Ben, I presume?"

He nods, his gaze roaming over her curvy frame, and his mouth presses into a smirk. "The one and only."

If this dude wants to hold Natalie's attention, he's going to have to up his game. His pickup lines are cheesy as hell, but rather than scoff at his lame attempt at flirting, Natalie only giggles.

The fuck? I narrow my eyes.

"Oh, and this is my friend Camden." Natalie places her hand on my shoulder and flashes me a quick grin.

"Hey, man. Nice to meet you. You're the new bartender here, right?" I offer him my hand, and he gives it a firm shake.

Ben nods. "Yep. What about you? You work around here?"

"I'm a doctor, actually. Pediatrics."

Natalie smiles warmly as I say this, and pride blooms in my chest.

Ben all but ignores me, his gaze moving back to Natalie.

And trust me, I get it. She's dressed in a pair of jeans that hug her every curve, and a pale blue V-neck top that ghosts over her breasts in a rather distracting manner. Every red-blooded male in this place has noticed her, and just because what we have is strictly platonic doesn't mean I'm the exception to that rule. She's beautiful. Exceedingly so. We've never gone to that place in our relationship, but that doesn't mean I don't know the effect she has on a man. Of course I do. I'd be a fucking idiot not to.

Ben signals the bartender and orders himself a craft beer, pausing to ask Natalie what she'd like. One point for manners, I suppose. She orders a second glass of chardonnay.

Wine occasionally gives her a headache, and I chew the inside of my cheek to stop myself from pointing this out to her. She's a big girl; she can handle it.

When their drinks are delivered, Ben leans closer, smiling as he asks her what she does for a living.

Natalie launches into an explanation about her work doing digital marketing for a nonprofit agency. It's a topic she's so passionate about, I feel my lips curving up into a grin. I've heard her give this same spiel at various outings over the years, but her enthusiasm for what she does never gets old.

When I glance their way again, Ben has narrowed his eyes and is looking at me. I blink and focus my attention on my drink instead. He thinks I'm cock-blocking him, but it's the furthest thing from the truth. If Natalie wants to take this guy home tonight, I certainly won't stop her. I might check in with her first, make sure she feels safe and has protection . . .

Shit. I scrub a hand over my face.

I need to butt out. I don't want to be that guy. This is her business.

Just because I've taken a vow to be celibate doesn't mean Natalie has. She's free to date whomever she pleases, as long as he treats her right. Picking up my drink, I plaster on a smile and face them. "Well, you two have fun. Nice to meet you, Ben."

I don't miss the way Natalie's mouth turns down in a frown. Then again, there's very little I miss about her—period. The way her hair turns golden when it catches the light, or the slight dimple in her left cheek when she laughs. Hell, even that fried pickles give her gas.

"You sure you have to go?" she asks, watching my eyes for signs there's something wrong.

"Yeah. I'm going to go talk to Jack for a few minutes and then head out."

"Have a good night," Ben says quickly, obviously happy to be rid of me.

Natalie's eyes stay on mine for a second longer. Gripping my drink in one hand, I stuff the other into my pocket to keep from doing something stupid, like reaching out and hugging her good-bye. Then she gives me a small, sweet smile, and something strangely possessive stirs inside me.

Let her enjoy her date. Don't be a dick.

No one wants a third wheel on their first date, I tell myself. This is the right thing to do. I stroll away, heading to the back of the bar toward the offices. The truth is, I'm not ready to go. It's still early and I could hang out, but the truth is, even if I hadn't made the pact with Jack, the last thing I'm in the mood for is looking for a hookup tonight.

I finish my drink in a single gulp, letting the alcohol burn a path down my throat, then set the glass on the end of the bar on my way toward the back hallway. I find Jack inside his office, his head down as he looks over a pile of invoices.

"Hey," I say, slumping down in the seat in front of his desk.

"What's up, man? You taking off?"

I nod. "Ben's here. He and Nat seem to be hitting it off."

"Yeah?"

I shrug, my look saying everything he needs to know. *Well enough to completely ignore me, so yeah.*

"Cool." Jack leans back in his chair. "You sure you've gotta go? It's early."

Rubbing one hand over the back of my neck, I sigh. "Got nothing better to do. It's not like I'm going to look for a woman to take home tonight."

He grins. "You're still into this bet?"

"Absolutely. No way I'm doing your laundry for a fucking year. I plan to win the bet. Easily."

Jack chuckles as I rise to my feet. "Have fun with your hand tonight."

I flip him my middle finger on the way out. "Ditto, fucker."

• • •

The next morning, I wake up early and go for a jog to clear my head. Unfortunately, the thought that pervades my entire jog is the way Natalie looked in her underwear yesterday, and the comment she made about not being fingered in forever.

When I get back from my run, breathless and sweaty, Jack is still sleeping. His work schedule is pretty much the exact opposite of mine, which works well for our living arrangement. While my days are filled with early mornings, his are dominated by late nights. We stay out of each other's way, and while we get along fine, having the extra space is a nice perk because it's almost like living alone.

I head into my private bathroom and turn on the water for a shower. Stripping off my damp T-shirt and gym shorts, I take stock of what I see in the mirror. Six foot two, a muscled physique thanks to plenty of time spent at the gym, messy brown hair, some leftover scruff on my jaw. I flex my chest muscles, pleased with the definition I see there, and wonder what Natalie sees when she looks at me. Does she see her buddy from high school, still picturing me as a gangly teen who hadn't grown into his height yet . . . or does she see me as I am now, a man?

I've tried to stop myself from thinking of her, but it's been fruitless. Last night, after I came home, it was hard falling asleep, wondering how her date was going. I thought she might text me when she got home from the bar, or at least before she went to sleep to tell me how it had gone. But she didn't, and now one very unwelcome thought pervades my brain.

Did she take Ben home with her?

As far as I know, Natalie's not the type for a one-night stand. But she has been complaining lately about her lack of a love life . . . so, who knows. There's one thing I know for certain—the thought of her sleeping with Ben makes my skin crawl. I remind myself what she said yesterday, that she doesn't sleep with a man on the first date. But there's always an exception to that rule, especially if alcohol and hormones factor into the equation.

Yet something inside me needs to know for certain. I'm almost laser-focused on needing to know what happened with the two of them.

As I lather up under the spray of warm water, I hatch a plan. Dressing quickly in a pair of jeans and a T-shirt, I'm out the door in fifteen minutes flat.

• • •• • •

"Be right there!" Natalie calls out when I knock on her front door a short time later.

I know I shouldn't care if she hooked up with Ben last night, but part of me—this weird, possessive part I've kept well hidden—needs to know.

Fuck, what's wrong with me?

When Natalie opens the door, I'm immediately struck by the sight of her. She's just come from the shower, by the looks of it. Her hair is damp and her cheeks are bare of makeup and slightly flushed. She's dressed only in her robe. The scent of lilacs and clean cotton floats between us.

I can't help but inhale the scent of her as she leans in close and gives me a friendly one-armed hug. I have no idea what kind of body wash she uses, but I vow to sneak into her bathroom later and check. And then promptly buy twenty gallons of the stuff. The thought of jerking off while surrounded by the scent of her is a mental image so vivid, my cock twitches and stirs to life.

Get your shit together, Cam. You're standing in the presence of your best friend, not a chick you met on Tinder.

"What are you doing here?" She smiles at me, completely oblivious to the filthy thoughts infiltrating my brain.

I shrug. "I was in the neighborhood." And then I hold up the paper coffee cup containing her favorite—a chai tea latte. "And I thought you could use one of these."

"Gimme." Natalie grabs the cup and heads toward her bright, sunny kitchen. "You coming?" she calls over one shoulder, making sure I'm following.

I pray that she's going to go get dressed. Otherwise, I can't be held responsible for letting my gaze drift over her bare legs and ample cleavage.

"Just let me change, I'll be right back."

Thank God for small miracles.

She heads to her bedroom, and barely thirty seconds later, she's strolling out in a pair of leggings and a faded T-shirt emblazoned with our college mascot.

"Are you here alone?" I ask, propping one hip against the counter while Natalie removes the lid from her cup and takes a small sip.

"Of course. Who did you think would be here?"

I give her a shaky smile. "No one."

With raised brows, Natalie scoffs at me. "Things went well with Ben, but they didn't go *that* well."

"So, you liked him, though?"

She takes another sip and makes a pleased sound, muttering something that I think means *yes*.

"You guys going out again?" I'm trying not to sound overly interested, but the truth is, I am curious.

She passes me the pastry box I brought over yesterday, gesturing for me to take one. "For the love of God, don't let me eat all of these by myself."

Chuckling, I help myself to a chocolate doughnut, knowing they're her least favorite. "Thanks."

Natalie selects a glazed doughnut and takes a bite. Once she swallows and wipes her mouth with a napkin, she nods. "He's taking me to that old vintage arcade later this week."

I plaster on a smile and work to keep my voice neutral. "Wow. I'm impressed. So you do really like this guy, huh?"

Natalie licks icing from her thumb and gives me an appraising look. "I don't know. But he's someone cool to hang out with, and I'm very single right now, so . . . why not."

My throat tightens, and I barely manage to swallow the bite I'm chewing. "Right. Why not." I talk with Natalie a while longer while she finishes her doughnut, but I'm left with a hollow feeling in my chest.

CHAPTER
Four

Natalie

I'm on the last rep of this set of sit-ups when my personal trainer, Mandy, pipes up.

"Damn, girl, where is all this energy coming from?" Her hands are planted firmly on my feet, aiding in the process of the most cruel and unusual form of exercise. "I usually have to coach you through these last few."

"Honestly," I gasp, "I have no idea." I finish off the last few sit-ups feeling strong, then fall back on the mat in defeat. Mandy reaches across the mat to grab my water bottle and hands it to me.

"Can I be honest?" I ask, popping open the lid. I don't usually open up to Mandy like this, but I'm going to work myself to death if I don't.

"Of course. There's no secrets between a girl and her personal trainer," Mandy says with a wink. I wish I had half the pep this girl has on tap.

"I think I'm just super horny."

Mandy laughs uproariously. Well, I should have seen that coming.

After a stuttering breath, she wheezes out, "Well, shit. Are you seeing anyone?"

"I'm not *not* seeing anyone," I say, which is totally a non-answer. Ben is someone, after all. Someone I may very well come to like with enough time, effort, and sex. Fingers crossed for that last one.

"What does that even mean?" Mandy's expression tells me she's not buying it.

"I am seeing someone," I say, clarifying. "It's just casual right now." I wipe the back of my neck with my towel and take another deep gulp of water.

"Who is it? Wait! Let me guess."

"You've never met him. His name is Ben." I chuckle. I wish I had more friends like Mandy back in school. Talking openly like this about "boys" is a new feeling. I'm having fun in a way I've never had with the guys.

"What? You mean it's not Camden or Jack?"

My eyes go wide as I nearly choke on my next swallow of water. "Cam or Jack? No way!" I shout, maybe a smidge too dramatically. "I would never, ever date one of my best friends." The very thought makes me want to simultaneously laugh out loud and shudder.

"That's actually absurd," Mandy says, and I can see by her side-eye that she's judging my taste. "You have two gorgeous specimens at your beck and call, and you've *never* thought about hooking up with either of them?"

I open my mouth to retort, but only a half-assed scoff comes out. Okay, she has a point. Why do I feel like telling Mandy everything? Am I really this starved for female friendship? Without thinking too hard about that can of worms, I choose honesty as the best policy.

"Okay, yes, maybe I have considered it once or twice in the past," I say, and Mandy throws up her fists in victory. So much energy, this one. "But now it's completely platonic." I watch my carefully uttered words go in one ear and out the other.

"I knew it! God, they're fucking hot." Mandy's eyes sparkle with shameless fantasies. *Hold your horses there, missy.*

"You've only met Cam, though," I remind her. He picked me up from the gym once a few weeks ago, a sweet gesture on a rainy day. "How could you know what Jack looks like?"

"It's called the matching theory," Mandy says, nodding along with her own reasoning. This is going to be good. "Beautiful people gravitate toward other beautiful people. You're gorgeous, Camden is a total hunk, so Jack must be at least cute."

I try not to snort with laughter, thinking what Jack would say to being called "at least cute."

"You're very sweet," I say with a genuine smile, placing a hand on her arm. "Matching theory, huh? I guess that's why I chose you as my personal trainer." Mandy flushes pink, her pale skin glowing under the fluorescent lights of the gym. She shoves me lightly. "All right, you flatterer! You think I'm gonna take it easy on you if you compliment me? Let's move on to the machines!"

It's time for leg work. As I lean back against the cushion, cranking out repetition after repetition, I let my mind wander. How funny is it that Mandy thought I would ever date Cam or Jack? Yes, they're both attractive men. And yes, we all get along very well. However, I can't imagine romance blossoming with either of those goofballs. It's not like they're incapable of it. Both have had their fair share of interested parties, especially back in college.

While Jack took healthy advantage of that, Cam was always too busy volunteering at the local children's hospital to commit to a relationship. His nights were tightly scheduled with hours of hockey practice, dinner with a side of schoolwork, and then volunteering at the hospital. No time for dates. Even when hockey practice got out late, I would always spot Cam's silhouette stepping down from the dormitory entrance from my desk window. Where was he going with a backpack full of books? Off to read bedtime stories to the disabled children who had trouble sleeping soundly. He's unbelievable, that one. While I was balancing schoolwork with trying to have a social life, Cam was busy being a real-life superhero.

As I push my legs against the weight of the machine, I consider how unlikely my friendship with the guys truly is. I grew up wealthier than either of them could ever imagine. They both have loving families with few-to-no complications, whereas my home life is an ever-evolving complication. The first time I told anyone about my secret, not-so-charmed life, it was to Cam.

"You really look nothing like your parents," he murmured one lazy afternoon during our sophomore year in college. We were hanging out in my dorm room, avoiding the paper we were supposed to be writing. The sun was hot, its bright rays streaming in through the window, casting reflective light off the smallest specks of dust. Cam and I sprawled side by side on my bed, books and papers spread out around us.

"Those are your parents, right?" Cam asked, concerned by my silence. I followed his gaze to the picture of me with my parents taped on my closet door. It had been taken on a trip to Argentina, their deeply tanned skin accented by their light, wavy hair. My own skin was pale in comparison, practically glowing against the outdoor light.

"Yeah." I tucked a strand of hair behind my ear.

Come on, Natalie. Is that all Cam deserves to know?

"They're my adoptive parents." There. I said it. To my own surprise, my voice was steady, like this was a fact I'd stated every day since I could talk. In reality, I hadn't told anyone in a very, very long time. I'd learned the hard way to keep such secrets to myself, sparing myself the prying questions of those only interested in the drama, not in me.

A quiet moment passed between us. Cam and I both turned to look at each other; me assessing his reaction, and him waiting for me to continue. Our faces were only inches apart. His dark eyelashes had caught the edge of afternoon sunlight, casting a shadow across his cheekbones. He used to be so clean-shaven then. I recall fighting the urge to run the back of my fingers across his soft cheek, just to test the sensation.

"I never met my birth parents," I whispered like a confession. I could have gone into detail about being abandoned as a baby and left to foster care for most of my childhood before becoming a Moore. But I didn't.

He turned then, staring up at the ceiling. I wondered if I had gone further than I should have in opening up. Was this too much information for our friendship to handle?

"Natalie Moore has a nice ring to it, though," was all he said.

And that was all he needed to say. He understood some small part of me, but didn't pry. Didn't sensationalize it or make me feel lesser than what I was.

With that memory still floating through my brain, I finish the last rep and peel myself off the leg machine with an exaggerated groan, feeling every bit as exhausted as I must look.

"You're getting stronger and stronger every week, girl," Mandy says, leaning over the metal bars of a neighboring machine.

"Thank you." I laugh. "It's definitely not a walk in the park. Hell, I'm not even sure I can walk out of here when I get finished with you, much less take a walk in the park." I stretch my warm muscles in hopes that they won't ache too much tomorrow. Never far away, Mandy hands me my water bottle.

"I refilled it." She smiles. "Ice cold."

"Bless you." I take a deep swig, letting the water dribble down my chin and onto my flushed chest. Mandy really is an excellent trainer, always prepared to lend a helping hand and listen to my latest complaints.

"I forgot to ask," I manage to say before taking one more swig. "Is there anyone in your life right now?" It's only polite to ask, seeing as most of today's conversation revolved around me and my lack of a sex life.

"Not in the slightest." Mandy rolls her eyes and her whole demeanor slumps, making me wonder if the peppy attitude she has during our sessions is just an act for the sake of her clients. "I'm just as single as I was back in high school. But back then, I wore a retainer. Today, who knows what the problem is."

"There's no problem. And there's no rush." I squeeze her arm in an *I'm sorry* attempt at comfort. I'm not very skilled in this practice, I realize. Most of the comfort I've shared with the guys usually involves a sharp slap on the shoulder and another strong drink.

"Easy for you to say," she mutters, her voice

colored in a new tone. Is that jealousy? "You have Ben. *And* you have Cam and Jack as backups in case Ben is a complete douche."

"That's not really how it works," I say, although I know that she's already convinced herself of the opposite. Before she can push back, her eyes light up with a new idea. I brace myself.

"So, Cam and Jack. They're both single, right?"

Uh-oh.

"Yeah. I mean, Jack just got out of the longest relationship he's ever managed. I don't really think he's in the game for anything other than some sleazy hookup." I internally cross my fingers, praying that Mandy isn't the hookup type. I really need her to stay my personal trainer. If Jack broke her heart on his lap around Rebound Town, the damage might be irreparable.

"Hmm." She frowns briefly, then looks up at me through her eyelashes. "What about Camden?"

Yikes. What about Cam? I frown. He's not with anyone, I suppose. I don't really think he's looking for someone. But what if he is? When was the last time I asked? And who am I to turn away an eager applicant?

"I don't think he's looking for anything right now," I find myself saying. Why am I thinking one thing and saying the other? It must be the workout. I'm completely wiped. I need a nice, warm shower and a long, restorative nap. However, Mandy won't let me stay in that fantasy for very long.

"Come on, Natalie, I'm not trying to be the mother of his children. Why not?"

Why not, indeed. I'm definitely thrown off-balance by this conversation, not used to this pushy side of Mandy. Sure, I like the Mandy who pushes me to reach my weekly fitness goal. But I'm not sure I like the Mandy who pushes me to set her up with one of my closest friends. This is what I get for opening up about my sex life, I think, reprimanding myself.

Taking my silence as a hint, Mandy's demeanor shifts again, and she scratches her forehead self-consciously. "Just kidding. He's way out of my league anyway," she says, sliding easily back into the friendlier version of herself. I bite my lip. *No, Natalie! Don't be this girl.*

"You know, you're right. Why not? I'll ask him.

Maybe you can come to his next game with me."

It's like I've resurrected the dead. The life jumps back into Mandy's face as she flashes her trademark smile at me, complete with perfect white teeth and rosy cheeks.

"What kind of game?" Despite her efforts at nonchalance, she's practically bursting with excitement.

"Hockey." I smirk, knowing that answer will push her over the edge.

"Yes!" She thrusts up her fists in yet another victory, this time for herself. "Count me in! Thank you so, so much, Nat." She blows me a kiss as she turns to skip back to the trainers' offices. She yells back over her shoulder, "I'm gonna get laid!"

Well, there goes the wind, knocked right out of me. I don't know whether to chuckle at Mandy's infectious eagerness to meet him, or to sink into the dread of my two worlds colliding.

Stop it, Natalie. It's not like Cam will get together with Mandy and then forget all about you. Jeez, I never knew I was the jealous type. I guess I've just never had to share my time with another female where Cam is involved.

I pick up my duffel bag and head to the locker room, my mind buzzing with questions that I can't even put into words.

CHAPTER
Five

Camden

I snap off a quick pass a split second before the other team's defenseman slams into me.

In the stands, Natalie laughs and says something to the blond-haired woman next to her. I grin like an idiot.

"Drinks after?" I mouth to her. Natalie knows I mean the bar down the street where our team meets after every game.

She gives me a thumbs-up, and I skate away to catch up with the team. After I hit the showers, I stand in front of the mirror, applying deodorant. Squinting at my hair, I debate whether to tuck in my shirt.

My buddy Greg, an EMT who plays defenseman, snaps a wet towel in my direction. "Is that primping for the fine-ass blonde with Natalie, or did you two finally add some benefits?"

"Whatever, man. You know how it is with Nat, and I don't know the blond chick."

"They're coming to the pub, though?" Greg tosses his towel in a pile and then shoulders his bag.

"Yeah, I think so."

He leans in front of a mirror, smoothing his eyebrows with a comical leer. "Well, you don't sound interested, so if I strike out with the blonde, then maybe your buddy Nat is up for some hockey-hero action."

"Get the fuck out of here, man." I laugh and shove him aside.

The bar is packed when I show up. Natalie and her friend have claimed a couple of bar stools and are fending off some smug-looking guy in a suit, definitely not one of the guys from my team. The blonde next to her smiles, but Natalie's mouth draws to one side and her eyebrows stay a fraction of an inch too high on her forehead. Polite but losing patience fast. That's my cue.

"Natalie, thanks for coming. Sorry, man," I say as I give her a bear hug that knocks the other guy out of the way and off balance.

"Cam, great timing as always." She pecks my cheek and gives my scruffy chin an affectionate rub.

Creeper dude huffs and moves down the bar, and I hold up my fist for a bump.

"Lifesaver." Natalie chuckles.

"That's what I'm here for."

"Mandy is a huge hockey fan." Natalie waves a hand at her blond friend.

"Mandy, nice to meet you." It's not that she isn't cute—she is. Just not my type. Jack would probably go for those big blue eyes and ample chest, though.

She shakes my offered hand but shoots an embarrassed-looking glance at Natalie instead of speaking to me.

"Cam, you met Mandy a few weeks ago. That time you had to pick me up at the gym? She's my personal trainer, remember?"

"Oh yeah, of course. Mandy. Good to see you again." How could I completely space on meeting her? My subconscious helpfully supplies, *Because when you're with Natalie, she's the only one you have eyes for.* Whoa, where the hell did that come from?

Our goalie, a surgeon, approaches to order a drink, and gives Natalie an obvious appraising look. I glare at him and clear my throat. *Move along, asshole.* I look down again to find Natalie and Mandy both staring at me expectantly.

"Hey, let's grab this booth over here," I say. "It'll be easier to talk." And in a booth, Natalie's ass won't be ogled by half the guys I work with.

I snag a beer from the bartender, walk over, and slide in beside Natalie without thinking. She nudges my ribs and flicks her gaze to Mandy, but I shrug it off. Mandy can probably take care of herself—she lifts weights for a living—but Natalie is way too sweet. And wearing way too little.

I mean, I've been looking out for Natalie since high school. No reason to stop just because she's a grown woman in skintight jeans and a top that shows a hint of cleavage.

I clear my throat and signal a server. "I need sustenance, and you ladies need another round. It's on me."

Mandy flashes a blinding wall of white teeth at me and then up at the server, a bearded hipster with dreadlocks in a man bun. "Gin and tonic for me. With diet tonic water and extra lime, please."

"Irish single malt on the rocks," Natalie says. When she tucks a strand of shiny golden-brown hair behind her ear, her mouthwatering lilac-and-cotton scent wafts my way.

"Give me another of the seasonal ale on tap," I say, "and a couple of the appetizers you have on happy-hour special." The guy blinks, staring be-tween Natalie and then me, like he's sizing up his chances. Jesus, it's a meat market in this place to-night. Not even the staff know how to act civilized. "Thanks, man." I hand over the appetizer menu to hurry him out of here.

Natalie leans away from me and settles her back against the wall of the booth. "Cam is the best pediatrician around, Mandy. You should see him with these kids. They *adore* him."

Mandy blinks at me expectantly, but I gulp my beer and try not to be annoyed. Natalie is trying to shove me in Mandy's pants, and every other dude in the bar is trying to shove me out of the way to get into Natalie's.

What the fuck is up with tonight?

"She's exaggerating," I manage to say. "I do love my work, though." *Ask the lady about herself, dude.* "So, uh, Mandy, how long have you been a trainer?"

Mandy beams and launches into a monologue about kinesiology and nutrition science. I try to focus, I really do, but that strand of hair keeps escaping to trail over Natalie's collarbone. It's taking every ounce of my being to not reach over and move that strand back to its rightful place. The appetizer comes, and Natalie slides over to grab a mini slider. Her thigh brushes against mine. When her blouse shifts, flashing a glimpse of the valley between her breasts, I swallow. Since I've gone mute, Natalie chats with Mandy again, both women stirring their drinks and giving me looks from time to time. Mandy's flirtatious, and Natalie is perplexed.

At the bar, Greg licks his lips and shakes his

head. His eyes fasten on the soft swell of skin that's currently giving me the cold sweats. He tilts his head in question. *Am I going to hook him up with my friend, the one I swore is just a buddy?* I glare at him and shove a piece of deep-fried cheese in my mouth. It's the bet making me feel this way. . . it has to be. Just knowing I've taken a celibacy vow has made me about ten times hornier. Nothing else explains the way my best friend is suddenly getting under my skin in the worst—and best—way possible. I'm so damn confused right now, and it's got me off my game.

"Cam. Paging Dr. Camden Carter. Did you take a puck to the head, dude?" Natalie's fingers snake through my hair as if she's checking for head injuries.

I jerk my head away and pretend to be fussy about my hair, but my primitive brain is apparently stuck at age sixteen. That special panic strikes me, the kind you get from a random, poorly timed boner, like on oral presentation day in high school. When she ran her fingers through my hair, my mind immediately went to her doing that while I was fully seated in her as she moaned underneath me. *Jesus.* How long was this bet for again?

"Hmm? Yeah, everything's great." I take a shot at guessing the conversation I was supposed to be having. Mandy's smile falters, so I assume I'm not even in the arena with that one.

Natalie gives me a concerned look. "Cam, you're seriously not yourself. What's wrong? I'm going to feel terrible if you really did get a concussion."

"No, I'm fine. It's just been a long week, and it was a tough game. To be honest, I'm beat. Sorry, ladies, I'm poor company tonight."

Their faces fall and soften with concern, and then Mandy's gaze wanders over to Greg, who's still looking in the general direction of our table.

"I knew something was up. You've been off since you walked in." Natalie pats my leg, and I try not to notice how high her hand is on my thigh.

Jesus.

"Nat, do you mind if we head out? I think I'm just worn out from this week."

Lies. All lies.

"Oh. Yeah, of course." Natalie glances at Mandy. They exchange one of those enigmatic girl stares, as if questions are silently being asked and answered within a few heartbeats' time.

"It was nice to see you again, Mandy."

"It was great to see you too, Cam." She holds out a hand for me to shake. "I'm sure I'll see you around. Hope you feel better."

"Do you want to share a cab?" Natalie asks her friend.

"No, I'm going to go have another at the bar. You guys go ahead."

"Are you sure?"

Mandy's perky smile is back, but it isn't aimed at me this time. I can almost see Greg high-fiving himself. *Good.* Better her than Natalie to get mixed up with that cocky bastard.

"Yeah. Definitely. See you Monday at five thirty, Nat. I'm going to bring the pain, so be ready."

As they hug, I settle my tab and pay for another drink for Mandy, feeling bad about totally forgetting who she was earlier.

Then Natalie and I head out, and I wrestle my

raging hormones under control yet again. After a quick cab ride, Natalie follows me up to my place.

"All right, old man. You owe me a beer at least for ending the night at . . ." She glances at her phone. "Nine thirty."

"Local microbrew or the watered-down light crap?"

"Don't play with me. You know what I like."

I pour a locally produced pilsner in a tall glass I pull from the freezer. She's kicked off her shoes, settled on the sofa, and tucked her feet under her. I lean over to hand her the glass just as she rolls her head to the side and back, stretching her neck. *Damn.* A mental picture of me sucking gently on that spot over her collarbone flashes through my brain.

"Is Jack working tonight?" she asks.

"Yeah, as far as I know."

"Does he have a rebound chick yet? I wouldn't be surprised. The bigger the heartbreak, the faster Jack wants to replace her."

"Nah, I think he'll take his time. For once.

He actually swore off women for a while." I walk around and snag the TV remote as I sink into the cushions.

Natalie lets out a bark of laughter. "Jack? Yeah, right. That won't last long."

I chuckle. "That's what I told him when he mentioned it the other night. Fucker actually got me to make this pact with him. No hooking up for thirty days. The loser has to do the other's laundry for a year."

Her eyebrows dart up. "Wow."

"Speaking of love lives, how are things with Ben?"

She takes a long sip of beer. The TV flickers on, landing on some manly reality show about gold miners or loggers or something.

Good," she says. "Yeah, good. Ben's nice; we've been out a couple times. I definitely have fun with him, and we have plenty in common. Nothing serious, but I mean, yeah. Things are good." She sounds a little like she's trying to convince herself.

"Well then, good. I guess."

On TV, a guy weighed down with safety gear starts a chainsaw.

"What about you? Why did you pass on Mandy?" Natalie leans to the side and bumps me gently, then prods my arm. "And believe me, you are seriously tense, my friend."

I roll my shoulders. "I don't know. I just wasn't feeling it with Mandy. But, yeah, I guess I am tense." I stretch my neck from one side to the other.

"Here, let me. I'll get some of these knots out." Natalie shoves at me until I turn around on the sofa and present her with my back.

"Shirt off," she orders. "Might as well do it the right way."

Because words fail me, I reach back and pull my T-shirt over my head. Her fingers are tentative at first, and then her palms slide over the tightly corded muscles and tendons in my neck. Her thumbs dig in, tracing firm circles in my flesh. The silence that falls between us is probably just concentration. Yeah, I'm sure that's all it is.

Her slender fingers work down the ridges on either side of my spine and then up over my delts. Her soft hands rubbing over my skin feels incredible. . . it has *definitely* been too long since I've felt female hands on my bare skin. Her warm breath tickles my neck as she leans closer. *Shit*. I clench my jaw over a groan as I realize with alarm that Natalie has given me a magnificent hard-on. *Fuck!* This is *not* helping any tension that I have in my body; in fact, it's only ramping it up tenfold. I could very well break in two, I'm wound so damn tight right now.

I try to be subtle about shifting the green throw pillow next to me over my crotch, but her fingers still for a second.

I lick my dry lips. My cock throbs. But then her hands move again, slower. The space between us suddenly feels warmer. The air I'm attempting to breathe in feels thicker. If there were any blood flow to my brain, I might wonder what the hell is happening, but it's all been diverted to the situation in my pants. The TV goes silent for a second after a commercial, and in that space, I swear she can hear my heart thudding hard and fast in my chest.

And still neither of us speaks.

Natalie's soft hands drift over my shoulders, her thumbs working into the muscle while my cock continues to throb.

A key rattles in the lock. Jack comes inside, dropping his shoes noisily with a sigh in the front hall. Turning the corner for the living room, he opens his mouth to say something but stops when he sees us. A funny quiver crosses his face, like the face you make when you spot someone making a fool of themselves in public.

"Hey . . . guys. I thought you were going out after your game, Cam?"

"Yeah," I croak. "We did. But we, ah, bounced. I was tired and the place was lame."

Natalie's weight shifts behind me, and she rises to walk over to give Jack a quick hug. "Sorry about your broken heart. Found someone to heal it for you yet?" She smirks, clearly referring to the bet I just told her about.

"No, I think I'm gonna back off, let it ride for a while." He looks over her shoulder at me putting on my T-shirt, and shifts his weight. I desperately think of baseball stats and my eleventh-grade physics teacher, a slovenly old guy who drank milk of magnesia like it was water. Anything to get the erection in my pants to die down before I stand up.

"Pardon me if I have trouble believing that will stick." She laughs, but it sounds forced. Something is off. Not since the day we all swore to be friends have we found ourselves standing around without something to say.

She walks over and picks her purse up off the floor by the sofa. "I guess you're in good hands, the both of you, so I'm going to head home."

Is it just me, or is her face slightly flushed?

Natalie and Jack share a one-armed side hug, and then he shrugs off his jacket as he heads to the fridge for a beer. I stand, hoping like hell the bulge in my pants is under control. My hand hovers behind the small of Natalie's back as I walk her to the door, but I let it fall before I touch her.

"'Night. And sorry I ruined your evening," I say, my voice low.

"You ruined my matchmaking too, you jerk. Mandy probably went home with some other hockey doctor."

"She's probably better off," I say, but I don't say why. Don't think it, either. But when we hug good night, and my arms tighten around her waist,

I let myself think about how good it feels. How good *she* feels, with her soft curves and round breasts pressing against my chest. My body wants to stay close to her, but I force myself to let go and take a slow step back, giving her space.

"Good night, Cam," she says softly, her eyes briefly flickering on mine.

Without a word, I walk her down the stairs and watch as she climbs into her black sedan, waiting until she's pulled away before I head back inside. When the door closes, I bypass the kitchen where Jack is standing and stalk down the hall to my room. It isn't just my bet with Jack at stake; it's potentially the two friendships that mean the most to me in the world. Whether it was that massage, or something different about Natalie, I've somehow found myself in dangerous waters. At the age of sixteen, Jack and I swore a blood oath that Natalie was off-limits, and since then, I've never even let myself see her that way before. It's not like we didn't both know she was gorgeous; otherwise, we wouldn't have had to make a vow.

I need to get my shit together, and fast. If I don't, I could ruin everything that's most important in my life.

CHAPTER
Six

Natalie

"C'mon, Cam. Please?" I rack my brain, going back to high school for something—*anything*—that I can hang over his head, or some favor I can offer that will convince Cam to be my plus-one to my parents' soiree tonight.

"I don't know," he says. "It's been years since I've been to one of your parents' famous parties. What kind of event are we talking about?"

"Small, intimate. Fifty people . . . seventy-five at most. Best bartender in Chicago, if that's any incentive. I just need to make an appearance and we can jet, I swear."

In the silence that follows, I cross my fingers

and fall back onto my bed, holding the phone. Talking to Cam brings out the preteen in me sometimes, the awkward girl who desperately wanted friends my parents didn't buy for me. If he and Jack hadn't taken pity on me, I might have never learned to socialize like a normal person.

"It's not a yes," he finally says. "But tell me again why your boyfriend isn't going?"

"Ben isn't my boyfriend. I mean, we're just not there yet. If ever." My cheeks heat, and I wonder why I feel almost embarrassed talking about Ben to Cam. He's been privy to every dating misadventure of my life. "He's not ready to run the mother-father gauntlet, and for their part, my parents would read way too much into it. Jack already turned me down on the flimsy excuse of having to work. You're my only hope!"

"You know, I should be pissed that I'm your second choice." Cam sighs into the phone, and I picture him staring at the ceiling in the defeated gesture he makes every time he gives in to some scheme of mine. Which is often. "I'll pick you up at 6:45."

"Thank you, Cam! You're a lifesaver."

He laughs, and a warm, fluttery feeling stirs in my stomach.

"Seriously, you're the best friend in the entire world."

"See you tonight, Natalie." His voice sounds amused, even if he is going for annoyed.

• • •

Because Camden Carter is just that way, he shows up at my condo right on time—wearing a devastatingly well-tailored navy blue suit.

I smile when I see him. "Thank you for this."

He smirks, mischief in his eyes. "Unfortunately for me, you're very hard to say no to."

"I just need to finish getting ready. Five minutes, tops," I say, running my fingers through my curls to tame them into loose waves.

"Take your time." He turns to watch me go.

"Help yourself to a drink," I call from my bedroom where I begin hunting for a pair of nude heels I haven't worn in a while. I fish them out from under my bed. A spritz of perfume and my favorite berry-colored shade of lipstick, and then I'm ready. When I emerge a few minutes later, Cam smirks at me.

"I have your favorite beer, bottom shelf," I say, noting his lack of beverage. He's just standing by the windows, quiet and contemplative.

His gaze still on mine, he shakes his head. "You'll need liquid patience tonight more than I will. I'll be your designated driver."

"You're not wrong," I admit with a smirk. He knows that my relationship with my parents is oftentimes frustrating.

Cam's gaze moves lazily over the dress I've chosen—black with spaghetti straps, in a mid-calf length that's hugging my curves a little more than I'd like. "You look spectacular, by the way. I almost feel bad for depriving Ben of the view."

My friendship butterflies wriggle. That's all these are, right? Because they certainly can't be actual butterflies. Cam and Jack normally pretend that I'm basically asexual, like they don't notice I'm a girl. Compliments on my appearance are definitely not the norm from either of them. Looking up at Cam, I just smile and say, "Thanks." I grab my evening purse as he ushers me out the door with one hand on the small of my back.

Fifteen minutes later, we pull into a gated community and up to the top of the hill where my parents' mansion sits, brightly lit. Cam stops his car in front of the fountain and angles his head at my parents' obscenely huge house.

"Ready?" he asks.

"Never."

"Too bad. Suck it up and get in there."

"Suck it, Carter." I resist the urge to stick out my tongue, but just barely.

I don't have to spell it out that coming from a family with money has major perks. Growing up, when everyone else was put in soccer leagues, I got to take private horseback riding lessons. When I was applying for colleges, I didn't have to worry about loans or scholarships. And when it comes to family vacations? Let me tell you, the Moores do it up right.

Only problem is?

I'm not a Moore. I mean, sure it's my last name

now, but only because I was adopted by Barbara and Nathaniel Moore when I was eight.

Cam knows about my struggles to fit in with them. I love my adoptive parents, of course I do, and I know how incredibly blessed I am. But sometimes, especially on nights like this with their country club friends and all the showy excess, I'm reminded just how very much I don't fit in.

When the valet opens my door, I meet Cam in front of the car, taking his arm and lifting my chin as we march inside like we belong here.

Mother's perfectly cultured laugh, tinkling above the crowd, trails off when Cam and I appear in the doorway, so I know we've been spotted. Within seconds, both of my parents swoop down on us with stiff-armed hugs for me and icy smiles for Cam.

"Lovely to see you again, Mr. and Mrs. Moore," Cam says with a manly handshake for my father, and a single beside-the-cheek air kiss for my mother. I have to admit, he plays the role well.

"We did hope you would bring a date, Natalie," Mother says. She raises one penciled-in eyebrow. "Unless Camden is here in that capacity?" Her face quivers, as though she isn't sure whether to hope for or against that possibility. Cam isn't old money, but she might be getting desperate these days. I am turning thirty soon.

"Italy agrees with you, as always, Father." I embrace him primly, ignoring my mother's question. Best not to encourage her less-than-gentle probes into my personal life. "Ah, thank you, dear," my father says, then looks over my shoulder. "Graham, welcome. Good to see you."

Father has moved on to the white-haired man behind me, but Mother snatches my hand as I try to slip past her.

"Do *not* leave before we have a chance to chat, Natalie. We see so little of you these days."

"Of course, Mother."

I hate the way they can make me feel ten years old again, and wonder if it's that way for everyone. One look from my mother is enough to reduce me to a juvenile—which is probably why I avoid them as much as I do.

Cam steers me to the bar.

Two fizzy champagne cocktails later, my jaw

finally unclenches. I wander out to the back patio overlooking the rose garden, chatting with Cam about work and the ridiculousness of my parents' parties. We lean against a wrought-iron railing in the golden glow of the gas lamps flickering over the travertine stone floor.

"That guy over there, the one in the light brown wingtips, used to look up my dress at these things."

"Sounds like a charmer," Cam says.

"And he married my number-one bully from prep school."

"So, people in your circle tend to stay close to the ranch, huh?"

"Not *my* circle," I say sharply. "My parents'. But yes, they do like to keep the money together. When it gets too incestuous, someone marries some minor member of the European aristocracy, or—very occasionally—someone from new money." I knock back the rest of my third drink and enjoy the warm glow spreading inside me.

"Natalie, how like you to be hiding in the dark," Mother says as my parents advance on me wearing determined looks. My father checks his watch.

"The roses are lovely this year." My best defense is always deflection.

"Well, it's terribly inconsiderate of you to make us chase you down out here, but that's no matter." She waves a hand, and the diamond tennis bracelet at her wrist sparkles in the gaslight. "When are you going to stop this silly little rebellious journey you've been on? You're a Moore, Natalie."

I open my mouth to speak, but my mother only continues.

"Not by blood, but you're a Moore nonetheless."

I have a hole in my heart that my adoptive parents will never understand, and a need deep inside me to prove myself, to make my own way. I love them, I really do, but it doesn't change who I am, and it definitely doesn't change my almost desperate need to make something of myself so I'm not just the poor little castoff from a teen mom. I don't think it's something they've ever understood.

"We have been more than patient, but you really must get serious about your life, Natalie," Mother adds.

I raise both brows as I meet her gaze. "I thought having a degree and a career was generally how one accomplished that?"

"You know what your mother means," my father says. "Most of your friends have at least one child by now."

Ah, pointing out how I'm still single and childless. Super helpful. "By which you mean most of *your* friends have grandchildren, and you want me to keep up. *My* friends have more to think about than breeding."

"Obviously." My mother sips her champagne and eyes Cam's tie.

"Is that all you wanted to talk to me about?" Heat rises up my neck and makes my throat feel tight.

Mother's tone softens. "We miss you, dear. That's all. You can be just as fulfilled with charity work. And then you can spend next summer with us in the Alps." This is all code for *Come meet the right sort of European aristocratic man to marry and have little trust-fund babies with.*

"My career is important to me, and I'm doing

good work."

"But you don't need to." My father looks truly perplexed. Men in his world work, and women get expensive degrees they never use.

"It's like you two don't even know me." My stomach twists, and a full-body shudder rips through me. "What good is all of this if I'm unhappy? I *like* my life. I don't want yours."

Anger shoots through me, and Cam lays a warm hand on my back. But I'm not done.

"This is my life, Mother. I get to live it the way I see fit. I'm happy." *Well, sort of.* The truth is, I'd love to meet someone, but it just hasn't happened yet.

"That's all we've ever wanted for you, Natalie, is to be happy." My father's brow creases in confusion, and now I feel like a total jerk.

Cam steps forward and lifts my mother's hand. "So lovely to see you again, but you'll have to excuse us. Natalie and I have plans later." He shakes my father's hand as my parents stare, and then he rescues me from the ivory tower. Or in this case, from the uber-expensive travertine patio.

He quickly leads me back through the party, hands his ticket to the valet, and places one arm around me on my parents' front steps as the car pulls around.

"Where are we going?" I ask once the headlights come into view.

"Somewhere fun. It's a surprise," he says.

"Will there be people there?"

"Nope."

Satisfied, I climb into the car and stare out the window at the stars. I hate that Cam had to witness that. Hate how I'm always at odds with my parents lately. Soon trees obscure my view of the stars, and I lift my head. Cam pulls onto a small gravel road, and I smile. A few minutes later, the car stops in front of the secluded lake at the far end of my parents' estate. It belongs to the township, but only the families with grounds bordering the lake have access. Since it's rarely used, we treated it like a private oasis up through high school.

"Wow, I haven't been here in years." I step out and inhale the earthy scents of fresh air and wet sand.

Cam comes around the car and grabs my hand as I exit.

"Me either." He pulls me to the weathered picnic table my father once grudgingly purchased so we wouldn't picnic on the actual ground, because who does that, right? With a flourish, Cam pulls something from behind his back and sets it on the table.

With a sigh and a moan, I flip open the pale pink box. "And doughnuts too? You are now officially my favorite person. When did you even get these?" I select a standard glazed to start and sink my teeth into the fried circle of pure sugar and carbs.

He laughs. "I just had a feeling about tonight. Bought these on the way to your house in case things went south."

"You know me too well."

"Your love affair with pastries isn't exactly a well-kept secret."

"Still." I reach for another doughnut, cake this time, and sit on the table with my feet on the bench. When Cam settles next to me, I lean my head on his shoulder. "You're a good friend." Comfort and familiarity warm my chest at his thoughtfulness.

Around us, insects chirp softly, and a gentle breeze rustles the trees. It's peaceful. And perfect.

"Are you okay?" he asks.

No one has ever asked me that. Everyone just assumes I'm okay with it all. That I'm not only perfectly happy, but also lucky to have been adopted by a wealthy family. And I was; I do realize that. But there's more to my story, and somehow Cam knows that. In a lot of ways, he knows me better than anyone.

I swallow, emotion making my throat feel thick. "Yeah. I'm fine. The thing is, they're not wrong, you know?" I say out of the blue, then polish off the last of my doughnut and lick my thumb as I stare out over the water.

"About what?"

"I want to meet someone. Get married. Have babies. Of course I do. I just . . . I haven't met the right guy yet. That one who lights my soul on fire, someone who knows my likes and dislikes without even being told what they are, who would hang the moon if I only asked for the stars, you know?"

"I know. And you will. I'm sure of it. Now, come here."

I scoot closer, seeking warmth in the evening chill. He hugs me close, and we gaze out at the horizon in cozy silence. After the tension of my parents' party, being with Cam feels like a security blanket. He's never asked me to change, to be something else. He's never wanted me to fit someone else's narrative. I have never appreciated the value of that properly.

The alcohol in my system slowly fizzles out except for a low-grade tingle over the surface of my skin. It's no wonder Mandy wanted to date Cam; he has a comforting presence.

Cam seemed oblivious to her flirting after his hockey game, but who wouldn't want to date a beautiful blond fitness trainer? I should definitely tell him.

Just as I'm about to, I decide that I don't want to bring anyone else to *our* lake. I'll tell him about Mandy some other time. I'm sure I will.

CHAPTER
Seven

Camden

"Pass me the sausage?" Natalie asks, her blue gaze swinging over to mine.

For one brief moment, I fantasize that she's talking about my sausage, or rather the sausage between my legs . . . then realize I'm being a fucking creep. *Get it the fuck together, Cam.*

I lift the lid to the pizza box and hold it open for her as she reaches inside to help herself to another slice.

"Thanks," she says, happily bringing the slice to her lips and taking a small bite.

I swallow and force myself to look away. "Anyone want another beer?" I ask, rising to my feet to stalk to the kitchen.

"Hit me," Jack says from his spot on the couch next to Natalie.

I take my time in the kitchen, lingering longer than necessary with two bottles of imported beer in my hands.

Tonight is a totally normal Saturday night for us. Beer. Pizza. Football on TV. So, why do I feel so out of control? Something has changed, and I need to identify what it is. Fast, before I do something stupid and make an ass of myself.

Pulling a deep breath into my lungs, I carry beer out to the living room, hand one to Jack, and settle in the armchair across from the couch. Natalie's eyes are on the TV, and Jack's looking down at his phone. I watch as Natalie peels a circle of pepperoni from the cheese and brings it to her mouth, chewing slowly. Then her little pink tongue darts out to taste her thumb, and I stifle a groan. She does the same thing with the sausage, popping it into her mouth.

I so do not have time for this. I've taken a vow with Jack, and I don't give my word lightly. I pride myself on being the kind of friend who keeps their word. What would it mean if I just threw all that away for a piece of pussy? Plus, there's no way in fucking hell I'm washing Jack's dirty boxers for a year.

I scrub one hand over my jaw. Who am I kidding? Natalie isn't just a piece of pussy. She's the sweetest, kindest, hardest-working girl I know. And she deserves a guy who will worship her and give her all the things she deserves—love, marriage, babies, the whole nine yards. So, no matter how badly I want her, want to kiss her until neither of us can breathe, it won't be happening.

"Has Ben asked about me?" Natalie asks.

I casually take a sip of my beer and wait for Jack to answer, hoping the answer is no, and then immediately feel guilty. For Natalie's sake, I hope Jack doesn't say something insensitive that will hurt her feelings.

"Haven't seen him. He's had the last few days off."

Natalie's gaze wanders back to the TV, but I can tell she's not watching the game. She's wondering why Ben didn't say anything, why he hasn't made plans with her during his time off. I remember back to our evening at the lake, and how small and sad her voice sounded when she admitted how badly she wanted to meet someone.

Jack catches me staring at Natalie, and I quickly glance away. "Crazy that Weston is engaged," I say a little too loudly.

Jack eyes me again. This isn't news. He's been engaged for three months now. "Have you talked to him lately?"

I shake my head. "Not since he called to share the good news."

We went to college with Weston Chase. He was a football god back then, but it was nothing compared to the outright pandemonium of becoming a pro-league starting quarterback. Unfortunately, he was drafted to Philadelphia, which means we don't see much of him anymore. I can't help but wonder about who the lucky lady is since he's spent the last ten years being nothing but a player. The player has been officially played . . . by a woman.

I keep my eyes on the game for a few minutes longer, watching Weston complete a perfect pass that results in a touchdown. But the entire time, I'm aware of Natalie, aware of her presence in a way I've never been before. I'm acutely aware of the way she picks at her thumbnail and frowns when the other team gets a tackle. Of the way her ample chest fills out her knit T-shirt, and how small her bare feet look beside Jack's.

And I'm more than a little aware of the stirring of my cock in my shorts when she brings her water bottle to her lips and takes a long drink.

I swallow and force myself to look away.

Natalie rises to her feet and begins gathering the empty pizza boxes and discarded paper plates from the coffee table.

"Leave it," I say, rising with her. "That's what Jack's for."

"Dick." He smirks at me.

"I'm tired. I think I'm going to call it a night," she says, ignoring me and carrying the boxes into the kitchen.

"You sure? It's still early."

Natalie nods. "It was a busy week. I'm just sleepy." She places one hand over her mouth, fighting off a yawn, which I find strangely adorable. "You sure I can't help you guys clean up first?"

"Positive."

She picks up her purse and cardigan from the counter, and then crosses the room to place a kiss on Jack's cheek. "'Night. Thanks for the pizza."

"Have a good night," Jack says, his eyes still on the TV screen.

When Natalie returns to the front hall where I'm waiting, I've picked up the empty pizza boxes and offer her my free hand. "Come on. I'll walk you out."

"You don't have to."

"It's dark."

We do this every time. She stands her ground for a second, but she knows I won't let her go out alone to the parking lot.

We head down the stairs and I toss the empty pizza boxes in the trash bin as we pass it on the way to her car. She clicks the button to unlock it, and the headlights flash once.

"You sure you're all right?" I ask, stopping beside the driver's door.

Natalie leans one hip against the door and gazes up at me. "I'm fine. Don't worry so much." She flashes me a sad smile, and before I know what I'm doing, I've pulled her into my arms for a hug.

I hold her like that—pressed against my chest—for a few seconds longer than is completely innocent, enjoying the feel of her soft curves against my body. Her scent is maddening, and I inhale as I hold her close.

"Cam?" Confusion washes over her pretty features when I release her and take a step back.

I swallow and take a deep breath. "Drive safe."

As much as I want to deny it, I can't hide from the truth any longer. I am full-on attracted to Natalie. It's not like I didn't know she was gorgeous, of course I did. I just never allowed myself to notice it. And now it's like someone flipped a light switch on, because I seem to be noticing every last thing about her. The way she eats, the sound of her laugh, the way she moves . . . and worse, I'm getting turned on by her with every little thing that she does.

What the fuck is wrong with me?

I want to punch myself.

Only once Natalie's driven away do I go back inside.

I don't even wait to hear what Jack says to me about the game because I march straight into my bedroom, closing the door behind me. After locking the door, I shove my jeans and boxers down, freeing my aching cock, and give it a long stroke.

A breath shudders through me. With the scent of Natalie still lingering on my skin, I pump my cock in quick, efficient strokes, forbidden desire rushing through my veins. Shouldn't be doing this.

Shouldn't want her this way.

But when I picture the way her lips parted on a breath, remember the way her hands felt on my skin during that massage—that's all it takes. I'm grunting out a curse as my fist moves faster, my release coming hard and fast. Catching the thick spurts of come in a wad of tissues, I feel like the wind has been knocked out of me. I'm breathless and still horny, and really fucking confused.

The only thing I'm certain of is that there's something very wrong with me. Because you don't jack off to thoughts of your best friend while your other best friend, who you've signed a blood oath of celibacy with, is in the next room.

I'm so fucked . . . and in none of the ways that I want to be.

CHAPTER
Eight

Natalie

"**C**ome on!"

I wrench my car key in the ignition for the fifth time. The engine sputters pathetically in response.

"Dammit!" Of course my car would die the morning of my big presentation at work. I bitterly remember my dad's words after I refused to let him purchase a brand-new car for me.

"You're going to get stranded somewhere in that piece of junk," he said. "I'm here when you change your mind."

No way in hell was I about to succumb to that temptation so easily. Now, facing the probability of being late on this vital day, I regret that choice.

I dig through my purse, searching for my phone. Scrolling through my favorite contacts, I debate who to inconvenience this early in the morning.

My finger hovers over Cam's name. I hesitate, remembering how strangely he acted the other night. Cam isn't usually one for hugs, but the one he wrapped me in was . . . intimate. It was pleasant, a comfort I didn't even know I needed, but so out of the ordinary for him and hinged on the edge of awkward for both of us. But how do I talk to him about it? I could just ignore the moment, but I doubt I could control my urge to ask him what's going on in his head.

Choosing a contact, I hold the phone to my ear and wait.

"What the hell, Nat?" Jack's voice is hoarse, as if he was deep asleep before I called him.

"I have a favor to ask."

• • •

Ten minutes later, and I'm on the way to work with Jack behind the wheel.

"You owe me. This is not in my sleep schedule,

Moore." Jack works nights, so the equivalent of me calling him at seven in the morning is the same as him calling me at two in the morning.

"I know," I say, squeezing his arm. "I really appreciate it." I look out the window and watch the buildings zoom by, hoping I'm not late.

"Why didn't you call Cam?" Jack asks. "He's more of a morning person than I am."

I'm not sure what to say. I don't want to tell him about the hug, and I'm not sure why.

"Don't you think he's been acting kind of . . . weird lately?" I'm not sure *weird* is the right word, but *different* feels too vague.

Jack frowns. "I haven't noticed anything. Why do you think that?"

"Just a feeling."

An incredibly distracting feeling, at that, and I'm not entirely sure what to do with those feelings at the moment. But right now, I need to concentrate on this presentation and get my head back in the game. After Jack drops me off, I'm still contemplating it and remind myself that I have to focus. This presentation could mean a promotion, and if I blow it, all that marketing research will go to waste. I need to move up in the ranks if I want to make a lasting difference in this business. Their methods are old-fashioned in this modern age, and I know my influence will put us back on track. It'll also help my confidence level lately after the beating that it took at my parents' party the other night.

As I set up the conference room, I make up my mind. No more thoughts of bizarre male behavior until after work. *Focus. I have to focus.*

• • •

"Well, that went well!" my coworker Janelle says in the break room. She's worked here longer than I have, so her opinion is valuable. "Your findings were so interesting. I had no idea that we could use social media in that way."

"It's pretty straightforward," I say, pouring myself a cup of coffee. "I just put the pieces together. I'm glad that it went well, despite how my morning started off."

"What happened this morning?"

I explain to Janelle my car situation. Being the superhero she is, she offers to give me a ride home after the day has ended.

"Are you sure?"

"Absolutely. At this rate, you're going to be my boss someday. Best put my time in now while it counts, right?" She winks.

I blush at the compliment. Nothing my parents say can ever make me turn my back on these good-hearted people. This is where I belong.

After work, Janelle drops me off as planned on the street just outside my condo. I'm walking up my driveway when I see something that stops me in my tracks.

"Cam?" I blink at the male form.

I'm completely thrown off at seeing him here, yet here he is, bent under the hood of my car. Despite the cool fall air, he's wearing only a thin gray undershirt and blue jeans. His clothes, face, and arms are streaked with black grease, evidence of how long he's been under there.

"What on earth are you doing?" I ask.

"Fixing your car. Jack said it broke down this morning, so I thought I'd swing by and take a look."

Swing by and take a look? This man is *covered* in grease. That's hardly swinging by or just taking a look.

"I was just going to drop it at the dealership—well, actually have it towed there," I say. "You really didn't have to do this."

"It's no trouble. I only had patients until noon, so what else was I going to do with myself?" His lips curl into a charming half smile. Who can argue with that face?

"Go on in," he says, ducking back under the hood. "I'm almost done."

Well, that settles it.

"Come in when you're finished and I'll make you dinner . . . after you shower, that is, grease monkey."

With a smirk over his shoulder, he says, "Will do."

Cam's hair is still dripping from the shower when he joins me in the kitchen. I've given him back a shirt he loaned me ages ago on a bet. I'll miss sleeping in the soft cotton, but it looks better on him anyway.

"Did you enjoy my rose-mint shampoo?" I ask, ruffling his short hair with my fingers.

"I feel like a new man."

"You smell like one."

"What's for dinner?"

"Baked ziti." I pull open the oven door and test the consistency. Needs more time.

"Smells amazing," Cam says, leaning in next to me.

"Could use ten more minutes. Let's go sit."

I lead us into the living room. Cam sinks into the worn leather of my sofa. I slide next to him, my old couch creaking under our combined weight. Before I can stop myself, though, I've wrapped my arms around him in a massive bear hug. We fall back against the cushions in a tangle of limbs.

"What's this for?" He laughs, pinned in my embrace.

"You're seriously the best. I can't believe you came over just to fix my car. Thank you."

"You're welcome." He wraps his arms tighter

around me.

I breathe in the scent of him—the usual fresh masculinity mixed with the smell of my soap. It's a pleasant combination. I'm so comfortable like this, resting here after a long day. I sigh happily, releasing the stress of the chaos of the morning and all the time spent preparing for my presentation.

"I take it we're going to stay like this for a while?" he asks.

"Yep."

A moment or two passes, and I feel Cam nuzzle his nose into my hair. I don't mind the feeling at all. It's comfortable. Familiar. Two friends just enjoying being around each other. But as soon as he's wrapped around me and smelling my hair, I feel the change.

Without warning, Cam jumps to his feet, and I'm left on the couch without a warm body beside me.

"What's wrong?"

"Nothing," he says. I know he's lying. I can feel it.

"Did I do something?"

"No, of course not." He says this, but he's grabbing his coat and heading for the door.

What is going on here?

"Cam, where are you going?"

"Home. I forgot I promised Jack I'd take him out tonight. And I've got an early morning, so it's best to get this night started as soon as possible, you know?"

"What about dinner?"

He pauses at the door, his hand on the knob. "Save me some leftovers?"

"Of course."

Then Cam leaves. Not thirty seconds ago, I was using his bicep as a pillow, and now he's gone.

The timer on the oven beeps, the ziti finally ready. Disappointment sinks in with the realization that I'll be eating alone again tonight.

Was it something I said? Something I did?

I force myself off the couch and drag my feet toward the kitchen. I can spend the rest of the evening second-guessing myself or simply take him at his word. I bet it has to do with Jack being lonely after the breakup. Cam really is a loyal friend. But once again today, I find myself wondering if it's just me, or if Cam really is acting strange around me.

I just pray that nothing with our friendship changes.

CHAPTER Nine

Camden

Natalie is quite literally killing me. She has no idea, of course. She has no clue that my body is suddenly keenly aware of her every movement, that my dick is in a near constant state of hardness whenever she's close. She has no idea that she's physically torturing me, no idea that I can't act on any of these feelings because the repercussions would be catastrophic.

Which is why it just about killed me that I had to rush out of her place after she cooked for me the other night. She probably thought I was insane, which is obviously better than the alternative. She can't know that I'm developing feelings for her. At the very least, it would complicate things, and worse, could end up ruining our friendship.

Not to mention I've taken a vow of solidarity with Jack. But it's more than that—Natalie is totally off-limits. We're friends, all three of us. The three musketeers. If she and Jack started dating, I'd become the dreaded third wheel. If they broke up, we'd all be forced to pick sides. Sex and friendship don't go together. Everyone knows that. This is the reason I've been avoiding her for a few days. I can't allow myself to do something stupid like make a move on her. And I have a feeling it'll only be a matter of time before that happens.

Natalie has to know something is amiss. After all, it's unlike me to go days without seeing her. But since I can't seem to control myself or my body when I'm around her, this is the way it has to be.

We've still texted, me hiding my emotions behind innocuous emojis and LOLs so she doesn't think something is up. I don't think she suspects anything is wrong. Thank God. It's just really hard to be around her right now, so avoidance is my only option.

I've just finished cleaning the kitchen after dinner when my phone chirps from my bedroom. Wiping my hands on a dishtowel, I pad barefoot toward my room and grab my phone from my bed.

It's Natalie.

Ben broke up with me.

I stare down at the words on the screen, and my heart begins to beat faster. Rather than reply to her text, I select her name from my recent contacts and hit the CALL button.

"Hey," Natalie answers, her voice flat.

"Hey. What happened? You okay?"

A long pause. Followed by a shuddering inhale.

Fuck. I think she's crying.

There's nothing worse than a crying female. It's my kryptonite.

"Nat? You want me to come over?" As soon as the words leave my mouth, I squeeze my hand into a fist and bring it to my lips, biting down to prevent any more word vomit from escaping.

Another stuttering inhale. "Y-yeah. Could you?"

"Of course."

Jack pauses by my open bedroom door and looks in, his brows raised. "That Natalie?" he mouths.

I nod, holding up one finger. "I'll be over soon. Hang in there."

"'Kay," she says before clicking off.

"What's going on?" Jack asks.

I roll my eyes and shove my phone in my pocket. "That jackass bartender broke up with her." Jack's the one who set them up in the first place. I knew after one look at the guy he wasn't good enough for her.

"Shit. Really?" He scrubs one hand over the back of his neck. "She upset?"

"She's crying. I'm going over there."

Jack nods. "Yeah. Good idea. Go take care of our girl. Better you than me, dude. Crying chicks, no matter who they are, are my kryptonite."

See, it's not only me . . . it's every guy's kryptonite. The male species is doomed when it comes to crying women.

I leave our apartment a few minutes later and

stop on the way to pick up a bottle of wine, a pint of Natalie's favorite salted-caramel ice cream, and a box of tissues. I have a feeling we're going to need all three.

When I arrive at her place, I knock, and no one answers. Then my phone chirps with a new text.

```
That you?
```

```
                    Yeah, I'm here.
```

```
Let yourself in. I'm taking a
bath.
```

Jesus, Mary, and Joseph. Please tell me she doesn't expect me to comfort her while she's in the bathtub.

I follow her instructions and unlock the front door with the spare key I have for emergencies, or for watering her plants when she's out of town. She has a key to our place too.

Inside, everything is neat and tidy, just as I expect, and there's soft country music playing from the wireless speaker on her kitchen counter. I place the ice cream in the freezer and open the bottle of wine I brought over, stalling for time, hoping she'll finish before I need to go check on her. Just as I've finished pouring two glasses, Natalie opens the bathroom door and emerges from a cloud of steam, wearing an oversized T-shirt, her legs bare.

Her skin is pink and scrubbed clean of any makeup, and her eyes are two wide pools of blue. Regardless of how fresh-faced she is, I can tell she's been crying.

She removes the clip holding her long hair until it falls in loose waves around her shoulders. I can see the outline of her perky tits beneath the thin cotton fabric of her T-shirt.

I keep mentally reminding myself that I'm here to comfort her, not to get my rocks off. Damn my wandering eyes and lustful thoughts during her time of need.

My cock perks up in interest. *Fuck.*

I bite down hard on the inside of my cheek, trying to rein myself in. "Hey. How are you feeling?"

She crosses the room toward me, and without a word, I open my arms in time for her to fold herself against my broad chest. She nestles in against me, seeking comfort, and I wrap my arms around her, holding her there as she takes in deep breaths.

"Nat?" I ask after a few minutes, perplexed over her emotions. She and douche-face only went out a few times, and she told me it was just "casual."

She lifts her head from the spot over my heart and offers me a sad smile. "Sorry I'm being such a girl."

I smooth the worry lines in her forehead with my thumb. "Don't apologize for that. You're hurting; it's understandable."

Spotting the glass of wine I left for her on the counter, Natalie grabs it and takes a long sip. "I know my reaction probably seems ridiculous. I mean, Ben and I only dated casually for a couple weeks, but it's just . . ." She swallows, her voice going tight. "I'm tired of being alone, tired of constantly starting over. I want to meet someone. I'm twenty-nine, you know? I don't want to be single forever."

I smile at her and take her hand in mine, giving it a squeeze. "First, twenty-nine is still young. You have plenty of time. And second, Ben wasn't the one. You'll be on to bigger and better in no time at all."

Her mouth tilts up in a half smile. "You promise?"

"I'm certain of it."

Natalie and I carry our wineglasses into the living room and sit on the couch. The smooth, tanned skin of her bare legs seems to go on forever, and I make myself study the covers of the home-decorating magazines on her coffee table instead.

"So, did you want to go out tonight to take your mind off things and get sloppy drunk like I did with Jack, or . . ."

She shakes her head. "I'd rather just stay in. I don't feel like being out in public right now."

I nod. "Whatever you want. I brought ice cream. We can watch old movies—"

"Or we could make a voodoo doll of Ben and stab it in the crotch."

I chuckle. "Or we could do that."

This earns me another small smile. "Why is it that you've always been so good with the opposite sex?"

My eyebrows dart up. "Me? I haven't."

Natalie rolls her eyes. "You have, and you know it. You have this *thing*." She waves her hand vaguely in my direction, appraising me with parted lips as though she's concentrating.

"A thing?" I deadpan.

She nods. "You make women comfortable. You're safe. Trustworthy."

I grumble something under my breath. She's wrong. I sucked at picking up women until about halfway through college, but then after I got the hang of small talk and flirting, I went through a string of one-night stands. Maybe that's what Natalie's referring to. "I promise I haven't always been good at meeting women."

She scoffs. "Sure, Casanova."

I chuckle and playfully give her arm a shove. "Remember sophomore year of college, when I enrolled in that women's studies class to meet girls?"

Natalie nods, her mouth lifting with a smile as though she remembers it exactly. "It was just you and twenty other dudes who had the same idea, and one very confused instructor."

"Exactly. Horrible at meeting women." I chuckle.

We fall silent for a few minutes, and Natalie quietly sips her wine. "Where's Jack?" she asks.

"He's working tonight. Just us, I guess."

She shifts on the couch, folding her legs beneath her. I know if I moved to face her, I'd be able to see the front of her panties, and that's not a vision that would contain the beast inside me. *Fuuuck.* My heart starts pounding, and I begin to panic at the thought of Natalie finding out I'm aroused right now. What kind of friend would that make me? A fucking creep, that's what kind.

Inwardly, I'm trying to subliminally send her signals that I really need her to put on some pants. But outwardly, I'm trying to act normal, comfort her, and pretend that nothing has changed between us.

While I flip through the channels, looking for a movie neither of us has seen, Natalie polishes off her glass of wine and heads into the kitchen to pour herself more, and brings the bottle back with her.

We settle on a dopey comedy that's already started, and she settles herself right next to me, curling into my side. She smells so good and the skin of her bare leg is so soft, I can't help but torture myself further by putting my hand on her knee.

Natalie downs another glass of wine before I find the courage to speak again.

"You want to talk about Ben, about what happened?"

She shakes her head, pours herself the last of the wine, and then pats my scruffy cheek with one palm. "You're such a good friend, Cam." She grins at me, her hand lingering on my jawline. "So thoughtful. So sweet. You're going to make some guy a very lucky girlfriend someday."

Her eyebrows draw together in confusion, and I begin to chuckle. "I think you might need to slow down on these." I try to take the wineglass from her hand, but Natalie drains the rest and then sets the glass down with a loud clink on the coffee table.

"You know what I meant."

I chuckle at her again. "I think I do, and thanks for the compliment."

Moving her hand from my jaw down to my bicep, Natalie gives the muscle a squeeze and my cock jerks behind my zipper. "I mean, why are you still single?" she asks, her voice slow and extremely loose from the alcohol.

"I don't know. Guess I just haven't met the right girl yet." The lie tastes bitter on my tongue. The right girl is currently perched next to me, wearing nothing but a T-shirt and panties, and my dick is hard enough to pound nails at the thought of pushing her back onto the couch and having my way with her.

Classy, I know.

Her hand drifts from my bicep, down the center of my chest, and begins petting—yes, *petting*—my abs. As nice as it feels, I'm terrified that she'll discover I'm hard. I lift her hand and move it back to her own lap.

Natalie giggles at me and pats my upper thigh. "Oh, Cam. Always the gentleman."

God, has she always been this touchy-feely?

When she reaches for the empty wine bottle and moves to get up, I stop her. "Let's slow down. No more of these drinks for you. Have you eaten tonight?"

She shakes her head. "Wasn't hungry."

"You'll feel better if you eat something." I grab my phone and order her favorite takeout, needing to get some food in her before Ms. Touchy-Feely comes out to play some more.

Undeterred by my attempts at propriety, Natalie lays her head in the center of my chest, looking down at my feet. Or rather, I hope she's looking at my feet and not at the obvious bulge in my pants that's now mere inches away from her face.

"I guess I just feel stupid about Ben. I mean, I should have known it was a bad sign that he never wanted to mess around. He just wasn't attracted to me."

I let out a snort of surprised laughter. "I highly doubt that." There's also a strange sense of relief at the realization that she didn't mess around with him.

Natalie sits up abruptly. "I'm serious. We went on several dates, but we never had sex. That's weird, right?"

Swaying, she falls forward into my arms, and I catch her against me. "Let's lay you down. The food won't be here for another half hour. Maybe you should get some rest."

Natalie doesn't put up a fight as I help her up from the couch and steer her toward her bedroom. When I help her onto the massive king-size bed, she curls up her legs, looking so small. I stand beside the bed, and she reaches a hand toward me.

"Lie down with me?" Her lower lip pouts out, and I inwardly stifle a groan.

I'm here to comfort. I'm here to comfort. I'm here to . . . As much as I keep repeating it over and over again in my head, it's not sticking. *Comfort* sounds too much like *come*, and my mind is officially in the gutter.

So, against my better judgment, I find her impossible to say no to and join her on the bed, leaving a healthy space between us.

She moves closer, her legs tucked up toward

her belly, and I catch a glimpse of her pink cotton panties. I hate myself for it, but I can't help my reaction. I immediately go rock hard. And this time, Natalie notices.

Her head lifts off the pillow, and she inhales a quick breath. "What's that?" she asks, her voice filled with wonder.

"I'm sorry. Ignore it and it'll go away. My dick's just confused. I'm in bed with a half-dressed woman." It's my attempt at making a joke, but my voice comes out too thick and husky.

Natalie doesn't laugh. Instead, her face falls as she looks at me again. "Oh, and here I thought it was for me. I told you, I'm just not sexy, not alluring enough. I wasn't for Ben either."

I place one hand on her cheek, drawing her closer. "Ben was a fucking idiot. And you're wrong. You're gorgeous."

She rolls her eyes. "You've never lied to me, Cam. Don't start now."

I let my hand trail down from the soft skin of her cheek, to her shoulder, arm, waist, and then finally to the bare skin of her leg. Natalie watches me with wide, appraising eyes as my fingertips move over her smooth skin.

What the fuck am I doing?

What. The. Fuck. Am. I. Doing?

But now that I've started touching her, the last thing I want to do is stop. I rise to my knees and look down at her. Then I push her T-shirt up out of the way, exposing her panties. Natalie doesn't stop me. She doesn't say or do anything, but continues watching me as her chest rises and falls with shallow breaths.

I trail one finger over the center of her panties, feeling the heat of her pussy through the thin cotton, and I almost moan.

"Cam?" she asks, her voice shaky.

"Yeah?" I stroke her again, this time right over the firm peak of her clit.

"W-what are you doing?"

I push her T-shirt higher, my fingers trailing over her stomach. "Showing you you're wrong. Making you feel better. Take your pick." My voice sounds deep and need-filled, even to my own ears, but Natalie doesn't pull away. She doesn't try to cover herself, or demand that I stop. Instead, she's watching me with a curious and lustful expression of her own.

I push her T-shirt up farther, exposing her bare breasts, and fuck me, they're even more perfect than I ever imagined. They're full and pale and soft, with light pink nipples that I want desperately to feel harden under my tongue.

Then she places one hand on my wrist. I haven't stroked her again, but my hand is resting right above her pubic bone. But she doesn't move my hand away, she just grips it lightly in hers. "You don't have to." Her voice is so soft, barely above a whisper.

"I know that. I want to. Now, stop talking unless it's to tell me to stop."

I pause for a second, giving her the chance to tell me she doesn't want this. In fact, I'm fully prepared for it, and ready for her to tell me to stop. We're crossing into new territory here, and I won't rush this. I want her to process exactly what's about to happen. But Natalie stays quiet, hardly moving except for the peek of her tongue when it darts out to wet her lower lip. I wait what seems an appropriate amount of time, and not a word comes out of those gorgeous lips.

Slowly, I reach for the sides of her panties and draw them down her hips. She lifts her hips, letting me drag the panties away, and I drop them over the side of the bed.

Her pussy is shaved and so pink and plump, I physically shudder when I think about how good it would feel pushing inside. But this isn't for me. This is for *her*, and the only thing I want is to make her feel good.

"How long has it been since you've been fingered again?" A small smile lifts one side of my mouth.

She tosses a pillow at my head, but I duck out of the way at the last second. Natalie is wide-eyed and watching me with a lust-filled expression.

I lower my mouth to her belly and place a wet kiss just south of her belly button. She squirms on the bed beneath me.

Kissing my way down, I take my time until she's rocking her hips in search of more contact.

I don't even think she knows she's doing it. It's sexy as fuck. My mouth finally makes contact, my tongue licking slowly along her wet flesh.

"Oh my God, Cam . . ." She moans, her fingers thrusting into my hair as she moves her hips up and down.

She's perfect. Soft and wet and so responsive. I could do this all night, licking and sucking and wringing these noises from her. It's even better than I ever imagined it could be.

"Cam." She moans my name again, her voice sharper now.

"I'll make it all better," I whisper against the silky skin of her inner thigh.

I push my middle finger inside her tight channel and let out a groan at how amazing she feels.

What the fuck do I think I'm doing?

I almost stop. Almost. Because this is insanity. But then Natalie makes a tiny, sexy gasping sound as she inhales, and I'm lost.

I'm helping a friend. That's all. Together, we're the poster children for friends with benefits.

"Your breasts are beautiful," I murmur, leaving sucking kisses up her belly as I move up to her breasts, my finger continuing to pump in and out.

Her body is practically quivering with need when my lips finally close around one swollen peak. I suck and lick one nipple as Natalie lets out a moan, and then move to the other, letting my teeth graze her nipple before sucking it into my mouth.

I don't know her body, don't know yet what will make her come, but for now I'm happy just to explore every inch of her that I can. I remove my middle finger, and God, I want to taste it, but instead I move my wet fingertips to stoke her clit in circles as my mouth continues worshipping her breasts. And then, without warning, she comes apart, writhing beneath me, making soft whimpers that make my balls draw up, my cock ready to explode.

Her orgasm lasts for a long time, and all through it, I continue stroking her swollen clit and kissing and biting her sexy breasts.

When it's finally over, Natalie looks up at me in wonder, her eyes wide and cheeks flushed. We're both breathing heavily.

The doorbell rings, and I realize the takeout I ordered for her is here.

"I'll be right back," I say, rising from the bed.

Natalie still hasn't said anything, but her gaze is fixed on mine. Her cheeks are flushed pink, and she looks thoroughly pleased. As I head from the bedroom, I have only one regret—that I didn't take the opportunity to kiss her.

CHAPTER Ten

Natalie

'm drunk. Not on the drinks I downed on an empty stomach, but on the sheer power of that orgasm. *Cam just made me come.* Silently, I test out the words on my lips, feeling how the sentence sits strangely on my tongue. What in the ever-loving hell?

I don't feel strange, though. *I feel good.* My hips are still wobbly, and there's a pleasant tingling sensation in my fingers.

I realize I haven't moved an inch since he left the room to fetch the takeout. I let myself take a slow, deep breath. My lungs quiver with the effort, and I feel my nipples perk up again at the memory of my labored breathing not two minutes ago. Those sounds I made . . . I didn't even recognize my own passion. I'm light-headed, struggling to gather my thoughts amidst the sensations of my body.

I'm unable to put into words what just happened.

It's almost unthinkable. Cam—my best friend, my superhero, my lanky-goof-turned-tank of a man—just made me come. I try to remember the last time I orgasmed so intensely. My mind blanks. I almost don't want to admit it, but this was simply the most erotic moment I've had in . . . years. Maybe ever. It usually takes nearly an hour for me to feel anything even *close* to orgasmic, and most guys just aren't that patient. It took Cam less than five minutes, and if I didn't feel like time actually stood still with him pleasuring me, it was probably less than three minutes before he literally rocked my world.

As I lie in bed, my T-shirt still hitched up so my breasts and damp sex are exposed, I sink back into the moment . . . the look in his eyes when he pushed up my T-shirt, revealing the cotton of my panties. The rumble of his voice as he asked for my permission. The sensation of his single finger running a slow line across my labia, seeking entrance.

The perfect curl of his fingers as they found my most sensitive, precious spot.

I'm wet again from just the memory of it.

My cheeks flush a deep shade of pink. I can feel my blood pounding in them, a remnant of my excitement and evidence of my growing panic. How can this be happening? I never, ever could have imagined that we'd be in this situation. What does this mean for us? *Holy shit*. I can feel a full-on panic attack coming.

"Natalie?"

Cam's voice sends a jolt through me. I shoot up in bed, covering my naked body with my shirt. My feet are on the floor in seconds. When I stand, my legs are as wobbly as the day I lost my virginity.

"Food's here."

"Coming!" I yell across the condo. The irony in that response doesn't escape me, and instead almost sends me into a fit of hysterical giggles, because I'm trying so hard not to freak the hell out.

My God, why did my voice sound so terrified? Maybe because I am a little. Dread weaves in and out of my heart, between the beats.

What is this single moment in time going to do to our decade-plus friendship?

I sneak down the hall, my feet quiet as a mouse's. I peek around the kitchen door frame, spotting Cam.

Damn.

The line of his back draws an alluring picture, his hips leaning against the counter. His short, dark hair curls slightly at the nape of his neck—a detail I never noticed. With his long fingers, he uses a spoon to scoop out fried rice onto two plates in equal heaping piles. Even from several feet away, I can see the masculine veins traveling up his forearms and hiding away under his sleeves.

I'm not sure which sight I'm drooling at more, the food or the man.

"Hey," I say, a little louder than I mean to.

"Hey." He turns and spots me in the doorway. "Ready to eat?"

I open my mouth to respond, but nothing comes out.

"What?" Cam tilts his head with growing concern in his eyes. "What's wrong?"

I can only shrug, words escaping me. I can't hold his gaze anymore with my cheeks burning like this. He takes a step toward me. "Hey, it's okay. You don't have to be so shy," he says warmly. I cover my face with my hands and groan. *Why is he being so nice about this?*

"Hey, hey, hey, come here." Cam wraps me in his firm arms and props his chin on the top of my head, surrounded me with the fresh scent of his cotton shirt. The muscles I didn't realize I was tensing loosen at the familiarity of the embrace. I know this man. This man knows me. Maybe this will all be okay . . . someday. I hope.

"I'm so embarrassed," I mumble into his shirt.

"You have no reason to be. It was no big deal," he says. "I just wanted to help. You seemed like you needed that."

"I did." I sigh. "I really did."

"Do you feel better?"

"Yeah."

Cam releases me and plants a quick kiss on

the top of my head. "Then let's eat something. I'm starving, and I could use some sustenance after that workout," he says, waggling his eyebrows. Here's the goofball I remember.

"Oh, shut up. You volunteered. Actually, let me put on clothes this time."

"Probably a good idea." He chuckles.

In minutes, we're sprawled across the couch again, shoveling chicken and rice into our mouths. Between bites, I tell him about how well my presentation went. He tells me about his new hockey practice schedule. It's almost like the last hour was a dream. Cam never fingered me, and it was all some strange, unfamiliar fantasy. However, the rush of endorphins in my blood is a constant reminder that something *did* happen. Something intense.

When he gets up to leave, I remember a particular detail I didn't take the opportunity to really think about until now. *His erection. Was that for me? And does he need a release now too?* He said it wasn't because of anything I did, that it was just a male thing. Still, as I stand, I wonder if I should return the favor. As a friend, of course. It's the least I can do.

"Good night, Natalie," he says, tucking a strand of hair behind my ear. I lean into the touch, enjoying the way his fingertips brush against my cheekbone. I'm about to ask him if he'd like me to, you know, *help* him, when he interrupts me.

"Thanks for tonight." With that, he's out the door. The condo feels empty now. I drag my feet back to my room and fall back into bed, exhausted from tonight's myriad of emotions. The sheets are cold now, no longer holding the scent of our sweat. But when I close my eyes, I can still hear my own whimpers as if they've bled into the walls and now echo back to me.

There's a sexy side to Cam that I never appreciated. Why would I? Now, it's undeniable. There's something incredibly enticing about the way he always comes to my rescue. Be it an emergency car fix, or something a little more intimate . . . There's no way I will be forgetting those few minutes anytime soon. There's no way I want to.

These best-friend butterflies are here to stay.

CHAPTER
Eleven

Camden

"Come on, don't be a pussy," Jack says, eyeing the barbell I've just set down at my feet. "You've got one more set in you."

It doesn't matter that heavy rock music blares around us, or that sweaty bodies linger nearby. My mind is so unfocused on this workout, it's not even funny.

I wipe my forehead with the sleeve of my T-shirt and bend down to pick up the barbell again, needing to pump out ten more reps of bicep curls, if only to get him off my back.

If Jack had any idea what happened last night, he wouldn't be this cheery. In fact, he'd probably punch me square in the fucking jaw.

But me? I'm still floating on cloud fucking nine. Part of me still can't believe what happened, can't believe Natalie was so needy and responsive when I touched her. And now this new knowledge that I have about my buddy Natalie is occupying every last corner of my brain—like the pale pink color of her nipples, or the gasping breaths she made when I touched her clit, or the way her body trembles and quakes when she comes.

If I'm not careful, I'll become aroused just thinking about it. And it's an unwritten rule that dudes don't get aroused in the gym. Jack would punch me in the nuts if he saw me sporting a woody while he's spotting me bench-pressing.

"You haven't caved, have you?" Jack asks out of the blue. It's like he's reading my mind. It's freaky.

"Fuck no. There's no way I'm washing your laundry for a year. I'll tell you one thing, though. My hand hasn't gotten this much action since high school."

"Roger that." He chuckles.

While Jack finishes a set of hammer curls, I grab my water bottle and plop down on a nearby bench in an attempt to get my focus off of what happened last night in her bedroom.

Instead, my mind immediately wanders back thirteen years to the memory of when Jack and I met Natalie. It was her first day transferring to a new high school, and she wandered alone into the lunchroom, looking a bit lost. As if transfixed by her long honey-colored hair, wide blue eyes, and the glint of her metal braces, he and I fell completely silent from our usual teasing.

"Who's that?" I asked. Jack's mouth hung open, but he didn't answer.

Seconds later, Natalie approached our table, still with that look of uncertainty that she wore so well. In my rush to rise to my feet, I knocked over my chair and it clattered loudly against the linoleum floor. Jack stood too, pulling out the chair next to his and offering it to the new girl. When she thanked him and slipped into it, he shot me a look that said *suck it*.

We only spoke for a few minutes, learning that she'd transferred from the prestigious all-girls academy down the road. Then Natalie rose to her feet, going to enter the lunch line that had now died down.

No longer hungry, at least not for food, I pushed my peanut butter sandwich away and leaned in toward Jack.

"Dibs." I smiled.

He kicked me under the table, his shoe landing a hard blow to my shin. "No fucking way. I saw her first."

"You did not."

"Did so. And she sat down next to me."

I pressed my lips into a line. That part was true, but only because I'd been so overcome, I'd been too clumsy to pull out her chair, and knocked my own over like a maniac.

Jack's mouth curled up in a grin, like he knew he'd already won. He and I had already been best friends for a couple of years by that point. I knew him inside and out.

I was about to come back with some quip like *may the best man win*, when I was suddenly struck by a realization. If one of us went for her, the other one would be pissed. We'd never allowed a girl to come between us, and I knew it would have the power to create a huge rift in our friendship.

Shit.

"Hey, you hear me?" the very real Jack standing in front of me asks, waving one hand in front of my face.

"Yeah. What's up?"

He blinks at me, his expression amused. "What's up with you? You're lifting like shit today."

He's right, of course. I'm in no frame of mind to be lifting heavy objects above my head right now. What happened last night changed me, plain and simple.

But unless I plan to completely fuck up the two closest relationships I've got, I need to keep this information to myself. Which isn't going to be easy, considering the fact that every time I close my eyes, impure thoughts invade my brain. I shouldn't know that my bestie shaves everything bare—yes, everything. I shouldn't have the urge to strip her and spread her out before me so I can lick her pretty pink pussy or hear those tiny whimpers that drove me insane.

I feel like I'm losing my mind, and there's not a damn thing I can do about it. Because this shit is all my doing, and it's that knowledge that fuels my anxiety the most.

CHAPTER
Twelve

Natalie

I haven't picked up my knitting needles in almost a year, so my dexterity is a little rusty. As fall is reaching its peak, I have already developed the holiday jitters. Always around this time of year, I feel the intense desire to deliver handmade gifts to my loved ones. My only talent is with two needles and a ball of yarn, however, so Jack and Cam have grown accustomed to receiving all of their cold-weather accessories from me.

This year, however, I'm going big. Matching scarves for the boys. Very soft, very warm. Hopefully, they'll be better received than the gifts I gave them last year . . .

"Natalie, I hate to say this, but I'll never use these." Jack sighed, holding up the purple potholders I knitted for him. "They'll just get dusty in the pantry."

I pouted, regretting all the time I'd spent picking out the right shade for his kitchen and practicing the perfect pearl stitch for durability. How ungrateful!

"I'll take them then," Cam said, swiping them out of Jack's hands. "My pots need some holding."

At the time, I'd been too fed up with Jack to appreciate Cam's sweetness. Now, I recognize my knight in shining armor more and more every day.

That settles it. Something lame and store bought this year for the undeserving Jack, and a beautiful blue scarf for Cam.

I smile at the thought of giving it to him, watching him wrap it around his neck and burrow into the softness.

He's going to love it.

It's the least I can do after all the things he's done for me. Just this month, Cam has come to my parents' terrible cocktail party, fixed my car, brought me doughnuts on more than one occasion, *and* helped out a sexually frustrated girl. I blush at the last thought. All of that, yet he hasn't asked for anything in return. Not even a hand job! True, I haven't offered . . . but still. How would I even do that?

Hey, Cam, remember that time you finger-fucked me so hard I almost screamed? How about I return the favor with a hand job? Or is a little mouth service more to your liking? Sure thing, whatever floats your boat, after all.

That's a conversation for a different time. I'd have to be extremely drunk or living on Mars for that to happen.

When my fingers begin to cramp and my mind wanders, I take a break from my knitting. I have plenty to do, what with the three of us leaving tomorrow morning to spend the weekend at a resort to celebrate with our group of college friends.

I don't often get to see some of our old college buddies, since most of them are living in different cities now, but it'll be nice to have the gang back together. Even better, I get to embark on this adventure with Cam.

And Jack. When did I get so fixated on the taller, darker, handsomer half of that duo?

I slip into my room to begin packing my bags. First, I need to brainstorm the different outfits I will wear. What will the weather be like? Chilly? Mild? Obviously, I need my bikini for the hot tub. Forgetting that would be a tragedy, to say the least.

After I have a few options laid out on my bed, I pick up my jewelry box to further complement my choices. Dumping out the contents, a piece I'd nearly forgotten about catches my eye.

The silver half-heart pendant necklace Cam gave me for my seventeenth birthday still has the same sparkle as the night he gave it to me. It sits comfortably in my palm. The outside of the pendant is engraved with a delicate lily-of-the-valley design. A perfume of the same name used to be my favorite perfume at the time. I lift the pendant to my nose, indulging in the fantasy that I might smell the flower's sweetness. That I might relive that fleeting moment on my parents' front porch. Even back then, tall, gangly Cam, who wore shirts too big and pants too short, was a charmer.

I place the pendant against my chest and clasp its chain behind my neck. It falls perfectly between my breasts, a simple reminder that I have many blessings in this life of mine.

One in particular I'm truly grateful for.

• • •

"Please turn on the radio?" I beg Jack in the car the next morning. We're twenty minutes into our two-hour trip to the resort, and I can't bear the silence.

"It's not even eight in the morning, Nat. I don't want music or talking or *anything* other than coffee this early." He pushes his sunglasses farther up his nose and then reaches blindly for his travel mug.

"Both hands on the wheel," Cam grumbles from the back seat. He's much more of a morning person than either Jack or me, so his grumpiness is peculiar. I peek at his reflection in the rearview mirror and observe him. His hair is messy, like he rolled right out of bed and into Jack's car. *He's so cute.*

"Hey, sleepyhead, you okay?" I ask him. I want to relish this side of him.

"I'm fine. Didn't sleep well." Cam yawns, rubbing his eyes. His hoarse voice is kind of . . . sexy. I wonder if I should tell him that to cheer him up, but then decide against it.

"Here, have some sugar," I say, passing him back a maple-frosted doughnut from the half dozen we picked up. I've never known what his favorite kind is. He always just eats whatever I don't.

He accepts the doughnut with a grateful smile and takes a generous bite. I want to know. I want to know a lot more about Cam.

But Jack groans again, flipping his visor down to block the sun, and I chuckle, rolling my eyes. Being the owner of a popular bar, his hours generally run from the late afternoon until well into the evening.

"You going to survive there, sport?" I ask, my voice chipper.

Jack frowns and flips me the middle finger. "Fucking morning people."

My gaze lifts to the rearview mirror again, where I expect a snappy reply from Cam, only he doesn't seem to be paying attention at all. His head is turned to the side and his eyes stare blankly out the window. The doughnut I handed him is balanced on his knee, resting on a napkin, and he looks deep in thought.

Something about that makes my stomach tighten. Unsure what to do with myself, I dive into another doughnut, if only to distract myself from the thoughts invading my mind.

• • •

By the time we pull into the resort pavilion, everyone has arrived. Meredith, Jessie, and Grace wave from the front steps, smiling brilliantly at us. I'm thrown back to our college days, watching the three bosom buddies conquer the dating field from afar. We were friendly back then, but never really friends. After high school, I was always a little nervous about befriending girls. I wonder how much they've changed, if at all. Sure, we've stayed connected on social media, and we exchange congratulatory messages when someone gets a promotion or has a birthday, but that's about the extent of it.

"Can we help with your bags?" Grace asks, prancing up to the car. The former homecoming queen is still eager to please, I see.

"Not a chance," Cam says with his signature half smile. I almost want to remind him he's in the middle of a bet with Jack that doesn't encourage flirting, but I bite my tongue.

As we check in at the front desk, I listen to Jessie talk about the new position she's taken on at work. The look on her face is lovely, full of what I imagine to be pure bliss. "I've waited so long for this," she says, positively glowing.

"That's amazing, Jess," I say as genuinely as I can. Jealousy truly is a feisty bitch. I hate that I'm irritated that Jessie seems to have exactly what I want—a promotion at work, and love in the form of her devoted boyfriend, Tyron. I would love to find a special someone to start a family with . . . a family that will love me and accept me without expectation. I haven't been so lucky yet.

Meredith, who hasn't yet acknowledged me, wraps me in a quick side-hug. "Hi, sweetie, it's so good to see you. Us girls are going wine tasting downtown while the boys go golfing. Tyron and Max are already there."

"Fuck yeah," Jack says. "I haven't golfed since the eighth grade."

"Where's the course?" Cam asks, slinging his duffel over his shoulder.

Grace hands the boys a map of the resort from the welcome desk, and they gather around.

Watching Cam and Jack interact so comfortably with other women has never made me uncomfortable or envious. So, why the uneasiness? Why the sudden weight in my chest? While both guys have taken a vow of celibacy, I can't help but wonder if mixing single men and women together for the weekend will inevitably lead to someone hooking up, and I'm not sure how that would make me feel.

"Come relax after that car ride," Meredith says, winding her arm through mine. "We have so much catching up to do. And besides," she leans in, "you have to tell me when the hell Camden evolved into such a sexy piece of eye candy!"

My cheeks flush red with emotion. What emotion, I can't really tell. I look away to watch Grace and Jack discuss directions over the map. I'm not perturbed by that interaction in the slightest.

But watching Meredith undress Cam with her eyes has me prickling up like a porcupine.

• • •

At the end of the afternoon, I take one look at Cam and immediately do a double-take.

He's all sweaty from golfing, but that's not

what caught my eye. What's intriguing me is how tall he looks standing next to the group of guys. I never realized he was the tallest of them all. Guess it's just something I've never thought about. It's not like I've ever made it a point to check out Cam. The thought is almost funny, but I can't stop my gaze from wandering the length of his toned body now. He looks particularly fit standing there in a pair of khaki pants and a pale blue polo shirt.

When he laughs at something Tyron says to the guys and pushes his hands through his dark hair, my lips curl up in a smile. Maybe it's only because I caught Meredith checking him out earlier, but suddenly I feel like I'm seeing him with new eyes.

God, Cam could have any woman he wants . . . so, why is he still single?

"You there?" Grace asks, waving a hand in front of my face and laughing.

"Yeah. Sorry." I blink and return my attention to the girls, who are now watching me closely. "Might have had one too many glasses on the wine-tasting tour."

Jessie raises her empty wineglass and grins. "Cheers to that."

Meredith struts over to where the guys stand near the valet since returning from golfing, and places one perfectly manicured hand on one of Cam's broad shoulders. She rises on tiptoe and whispers something in his ear. Cam looks down at her and lets out a deep laugh.

Something low in my spine tingles.

"How in the fuck is that boy still single?" Jessie asks, shaking her head.

Grace gives me an appraising look. "You and Cam never—" When I swing my head around at her, she snaps her mouth shut, catching herself.

Cam and me? No. That would be insane. Wouldn't it?

Only now am I starting to wonder why we've never hooked up.

I open my mouth to respond as Meredith strolls back to the group.

"Okay, girlies, the plan is that we grab a bite to eat before we shower and rest for an hour, and then we'll meet back up at the fire pit by the lake."

"Sounds perfect," Grace says.

My heart is still lodged in my throat as I nod and follow them down the stone-paved trail that leads to our hotel rooms.

CHAPTER
Thirteen

Camden

S tanding in the shower under the heavy downfall of water is a relief to my aching head. After spending the afternoon traipsing around an expansive golf course with my college brothers, I'm much more tired than I expected. Golf has never been my favorite sport. Too much walking, too little game. I prefer the excitement of hockey.

I remember the beaming smile on Natalie's face from the bleachers at my last game. Her enthusiasm is always infectious, making me play harder, move faster. I wonder what she's been up to all day. A wine tasting isn't exactly up her alley either, but I hope she had a decent time. Maybe the wine helped her loosen up and shake some of those nerves she always has around her female friends.

In retrospect, I shouldn't complain. Spending the day catching up with the guys has been great. We've easily fallen back into our easy banter from college, giving each other shit for every missed hole. It's equal parts hilarious and exhausting, but I'm willing to expend that energy because I don't get to see the guys very often anymore.

I turn off the shower and rub my wet hair with the towel as I drip onto the tile floor. As I wrap the towel around my hips and exit the bathroom, I spot the time on the alarm clock next to my bed. It's almost time to join everyone around the bonfire. After that, we're dedicating the night to decompressing in the hot tub. The shower didn't soothe this headache I've been carrying around with me all day, so hopefully relaxing in the warm water will.

I dig through my luggage, pulling out a pair of trunks I bought on my last mall run with Natalie.

"Navy blue is your color," she said, tossing them at me. That was all I needed to purchase them. Yet another aspect of my life Natalie has had an influence on.

Will there ever be a day that I don't associate

her with everything around me?

God, I hope so.

I leave the trunks on my bed and dress for the bonfire in a pair of jeans and a shirt. After I push a little product through my still-damp hair, I head out the door with my thoughts as my only company.

When I arrive at the clearing at the back of the resort, the fire hasn't been lit yet. Grace and Meredith are already lounging around the stone pit.

"Hi, Cam." Meredith smiles. She's in her bikini top and sweat pants, a loose cardigan draped over her shoulders in a feeble attempt to ward off the cold. The temperature is too low to be so scantily clad, in my opinion. By the way she squeezes her breasts together and smiles at me, I don't think she's thinking about the weather.

"How was golfing?" Grace asks, genuinely interested. She's more practically dressed in her oversized plain sweater, leggings, and long socks.

"It was fun," I say, half lying. "Want me to get the fire going?"

"Such a gentleman," Meredith purrs.

The resort employees have already stocked the wood and kindling. I crouch over the pit and begin building the foundation for our fire.

"Where is Natalie?"

I regret the question immediately as both of their faces fall. I can't help but wear my heart on my sleeve, I guess.

"I don't know," Meredith says, leaning back in her chair with a luxurious stretch. "Probably with Jack, right?"

"Oh! Are they together?" Grace asks. I can tell that by *together* she doesn't just mean by proximity.

"Ask Cam," Meredith says, turning the question over to me. I don't like the way she looks at me, egging me on.

"They definitely aren't," I say, but these two women and their questions have me feeling ridiculously uncomfortable. In college, they didn't speak to me at all unless Jack was by my side. I guess me spending ten hours at the gym every week has changed their perspective. That, or the certificate from med school that places the letters MD behind my name might have a thing or two to do with their attention. Of course, none of that would matter to them if they had any idea how emotionally unavailable I actually am.

"You never know," Meredith says, poking Grace in the side, and she yelps. "Oh my God, stop, you know I'm ticklish," Grace cries. More shoving and groping commences. The squealing is unbearable, like poking sharp needles into my already aching head.

I'm glad I have a task so I can reasonably ignore these women. Were they always this annoying back in college? I guess Natalie had an obvious point every time she avoided hanging out with them. Speaking of which . . . *Where is Natalie?*

Is she with Jack? In one of their hotel rooms? The thought of that scenario makes my mind wander in all sorts of improbable directions. I've never thought about it before. Is it possible that they could ever have feelings for each other? The idea seems absurd to me, but a month ago I would have thought my having feelings for Natalie would be preposterous.

My stomach is twisting in knots. I grip the kindling with my hands, tossing it on top of the pile of firewood. Goddamn, I need to get over this woman before just the mention of her name destroys me.

"Hey!"

Speak of the devil. I can't help but feel relieved when I turn around to see Natalie, without Jack. She has a tote bag slung over her shoulder and wears a droopy knit sweater with yoga pants and fuzzy boots. The sight of Natalie in her comfy clothes sends a rush of emotion through me. Those are the clothes she wears when it's just her and me, hanging out on her couch, watching bad movies. There's nothing special about those clothes, but that's exactly what makes them special. Now everyone is going to see Natalie as herself, perfect and unassumingly beautiful. I swallow the sour taste in my mouth before I can admit to myself how jealous I am.

"You look cute," Meredith says.

"Thanks." Natalie laughs, pulling at her sweater. "It's what I brought to sleep in."

"Come sit!" Grace says, patting the chair next to her. That's my cue to take off.

"I'm going to grab some lighter fluid from the deck," I say, breezing past Natalie.

"Wait up!" She follows right behind, but I don't let myself slow down. When we're a few paces away from the others, I feel her hand wrap around my wrist. My heart throbs uncomfortably.

"I have something for you," she says, and I can hear the smile in her voice. I don't want to look at her, but I have to.

Goddammit.

Her eyes are mesmerizing in this early evening light. They sparkle more than the lake, a far inferior sight in comparison. Her cheeks are still rosy, I assume from the wine tour of this afternoon. I wonder if her lips taste like merlot. Before I can dip down for a taste, her gaze drops to her tote bag.

"I've been waiting all day to give this to you. I couldn't find the right moment, but what the hell, right?"

From the depths of her bag, Natalie pulls out a long knitted scarf. The colors are dark green and blue, reminiscent of the colors of the lake and the trees surrounding it. I know without her having to say it that she made it herself.

She reaches up and wraps the scarf around my neck. "Happy Christmas," she whispers.

I smirk. "Christmas isn't for almost two months."

"I got too excited." She chuckles.

I can't help but smile. The scarf feels gloriously soft against my neck. I can already feel it retaining my heat on this chilly night.

Her hands hold the ends of the scarf against my chest, and she smiles up at me. Has she ever been more beautiful?

"Thank you," I murmur, my eyes locked onto her lips.

"You are so welcome," she whispers. Is that a blush on her cheeks, or is it just my imagination working overtime? I must be silent for too long because Natalie speaks again.

"Where's that lighter fluid?"

"Who knows. I just needed a break from the gossip girls."

"Oh, please! You didn't have to spend all afternoon with them."

"How was that?" I'll keep asking Natalie questions all night if it will keep her hands on my chest like this.

"You know . . . really not my thing." She rolls her eyes. "How was golf?"

"Golf." I shrug, and she laughs.

"At least there's a hot tub," she says with a smirk.

"At least."

"Hey!" We both turn abruptly, and Natalie removes her hands from my chest. Tyron and Jessie are jogging up the hill to us from the lakeside, smiling wide.

"He fucking proposed!" Jessie screams, tackling Natalie in a bear hug.

"Congratulations!"

"Finally," I say, reaching out to shake Tyron's hand. He grins, grasping my hand firmly.

"Had to be right, my brother. Had to be right."

I can relate with that.

Natalie's eyes sparkle as she inspects Jessie's ring. "My God, Tyron, this is beautiful!"

"Isn't it?" Jessie squeals, wiping fresh tears from her eyes.

"Let's go show everyone else," Natalie says, squeezing Jessie's hand.

"What's the commotion?"

Jack hops down from the deck with Max close behind. The whole brigade is here. My headache couldn't be worse. Now isn't the time for personal insecurities and desires to get the better of me. Now is the time to celebrate two friends in love.

Must be nice.

• • •

After we're suitably warmed from the beer and wine, we abandon the bonfire for the hot tub. I've retreated to my room to put on my swim trunks. Apparently, I'm faster than everyone else, because I'm the first one back at the hot tub.

Or not.

Through the steam tendrils rising from the bubbling water, I see that Natalie is already in the tub, her head leaning lazily back on the cobblestone edge. Her breasts peek alluringly out of the water, small circles of soft pale flesh. A single line of sweat runs down her neck, diving into the crevice of her pale lavender bikini top.

She must hear me approaching because she opens her eyes. Her face is flushed, like she's just had the most exquisite fuck of her life.

"This is incredible," she murmurs, her voice pure sex.

Jesus. Just the sound of her voice makes my cock perk up in interest. I need to get in the water fast before Natalie can see how tented my trunks are.

I slide into the hot tub, the warm water rushing up around me. The bubbles tickle my balls, and I grit my teeth. I need no more stimulation down there, as it is.

Jesus, Cam. Keep it together.

"Are you okay?" Natalie asks, leaning toward me. Her bathing suit dips low. She isn't even aware that one of her breasts is threatening to spill out. She's more concerned about me. I don't know if I'm more attracted to her body or her personality right now. My dick is hard as a rock under the bubbling water.

"Oh, fuck yes!" Jack calls, grinning as he whips off his T-shirt.

Before I can answer Natalie, Jack hops into the water with us. I'm grateful for the waves he causes, further obscuring my erect cock. I've been so preoccupied with Natalie, I didn't even hear him or the others approach. They all stumble in, fairly tipsy. Everyone groans in delight at the sensation of the water bubbling around their arms and legs.

The conversation naturally centers around Tyron and Jessie's wedding plans, but I can't keep track of who is talking or what is being said. All I can do is try not to be too bothered by the sight in front of me.

Jack sits flush against Natalie. Her head is propped comfortably against his shoulder, her breast grazing his arm. They look so comfortable like that, a man and woman completely at ease with each other.

God, I'm so pathetic. Just the sight of them being cozy has my heart sinking and my stomach cramping with so many mixed emotions.

I can't fucking do this.

"Where do you think you're going?" Meredith asks, grabbing my arm as I get up to leave the water.

"I'm tired," I say, not exactly lying. "I think it's time for me to turn in."

"I feel that," Max says with a yawn, and I'm grateful for the backup.

"Okay." Meredith sighs, releasing me.

Both of my feet are on dry land now. If only my libido wasn't still skyrocketing, this would be a nice ending to a stressful night. I wrap my towel around my dripping body as quickly as possible and head back into the resort. I refuse to look over my shoulder. I can feel Natalie's concerned eyes boring holes into my back.

Don't look at me, Natalie. I promise, you won't like what you see.

CHAPTER
Fourteen

Natalie

"Well, that was weird," Meredith grumbles, clearly disappointed that Cam called it quits so early.

"I hope he's okay," Grace adds. Tyron, on the other hand, is completely unconcerned by the moment's drama.

"We were walking around that course for hours today," he says with a stretch. "A man can be tired."

This seems to appease everyone else in the hot tub. Still, I can't shake the feeling that something about Cam is off. There's simply no denying that his behavior is unusual. I sneak a glance at Jack, and he returns the look. We're in agreement. This doesn't feel right.

"I'm pretty tired myself," I announce to the group. I stand and let the water drip off my body before reaching for my towel.

"Oh, come on! You too?" Jessie whines. I'm distressing the bride-to-be, but the well-being of my best friend is a far higher priority.

"Yeah, all that wine and the bubbles and warmth of the hot tub have made me sleepy," I say, forcing a small yawn to convey exhaustion. I don't stick around long enough to see if they buy it. With my towel tucked tightly under my arms, I slip my feet into my flip-flops and enter the resort, then tiptoe down the hall.

Knockity-knock-knock.

"Cam?"

After a few moments of silence, I hear footsteps. The door opens. Cam, fresh out of the shower, stands in the doorway wearing nothing but a towel around his waist. I keep my eyes locked on his, so as not to dwell on the broad expanse of his shoulders or the perfectly defined muscles of his abs. *Focus, Natalie.*

"What's up?" he asks.

"Can I come in?"

He hesitates. Then after a second, he opens the door a few inches wider, allowing me to step inside. The door clicks softly behind me.

"Are you okay?" I ask, tempted to reach out and place a hand on his arm. The toned muscle there is tempting to touch, but I should respect his boundaries.

Shouldn't I?

"I'm fine," he says curtly, and we both know he's lying. I wait for him to change his mind, to try again—this time with a better choice of words. He's silent, his eyes as empty as the air between us.

"Will you talk to me?"

"Honestly, Natalie. I'm just tired."

Cam says this, and I would believe him except for the strain in his voice. What has him looking so tortured?

Or who?

"Thanks again for the scarf," he says when I'm silent. "I really love it." His smile doesn't quite reach his eyes, as if he's trying to appear cheerful but doesn't have it in him. It's not that I don't believe he's grateful. I just don't believe he's happy.

"You're welcome," I say, but I don't care about the stupid scarf right now. I care about *him*.

"You should get back to everyone else." When he opens the door and waits for me to step through, I don't move, refusing to take the cue to leave him. I don't want to leave him.

I want to hold him.

I take a step toward him and wrap my arms around his waist, pressing my body into his familiar scent, his familiar warmth. He releases the door, but he doesn't wrap his arms around me. They hang at his sides, unmoving.

Why?

Still, I won't let him go. I only hold him tighter. Burying my nose in the soft skin of his chest, I listen closely to the sound of his heart. It's pounding like a fist against a door, begging to be opened.

What happens if I open it?

Oh. The answer to that question is pressing into my stomach, a rock-hard reminder of our nearly bare bodies. Is this really just a male reaction again? He *has* to feel this too. This kinetic energy between us. This undeniable pull. I don't know what's happening, but it's something huge.

I look up at Cam and meet his eyes, brimming with secrets. I need answers, and I need them now.

No more secrets, Cam.

"What's going on?"

The man in my arms doesn't answer with his words. Instead, he takes hold of the edge of my towel and pulls it from my body. I gasp at the sensation of our skin pressing intimately together. I brace myself against his chiseled arms, digging my fingers into his biceps for purchase.

He isn't done. He lifts his hands, one to my hip, one to my cheek. His thumb draws a small circle on my exposed hip bone. With the side of his knuckle, he traces the outline of my lower lip. I stay very, very still so he won't notice the slight shudder racing down my spine.

"I can't tell you," he says so softly that it breaks my heart.

"Yes, you can." I barely recognize my own

voice. Cam's eyes, dark and hurting, are locked on my lips. I want to ease that pain.

And I think I know how.

I lean in closer, pulling myself up to his level with my hands on his chest. Our breaths mingle and everything is warm, the air between us aflame.

"You're killing me." These are the words that fall from Cam's lips before they meet mine.

God.

My lips are locked against his in the softest of kisses. I catch his lower lip with my own, pressing every ounce of my feelings into him. Every *thank you* for being there for me. Every *you're perfect* for being exactly what I need.

Can he feel how much I care for him?

He's still for a whole Mississippi second—a second too long for me to bear.

Oh God. What have I done?

But the moment I pull away, Cam leans in. His hands are on my face, holding my lips against his. He tilts my head, digs his fingers into my hair, and opens his mouth to mine.

"Natalie . . ."

The sound of my name slipping so lustfully from the back of his throat sends a jolt all the way down. *All* the way down.

I pull myself even higher on my toes, clinging to him with my arms around his neck. He returns the favor, wrapping his arms around my waist and pulling me tight against him. Our mouths are magnetic, unable to separate, unwilling to stop.

My God. I'm kissing Cam.

I'm kissing my best friend.

I'm kissing him and I can't stop.

I dart my tongue between his lips, caressing the underside of his upper lip. He growls, maddened by my bold move. His fingers blaze fiery trails down my neck and shoulders. His hands explore me, memorizing the slope of my back and the curve of my hips. Each touch is so soft, yet so electric.

Soon it's all frantic kisses and eager moans that I'm pretty sure are coming from me. I press into his shoulders, leaving handprints on his chest. My fingers draw lines down his abdomen, then finally trace along the bulge beneath his towel.

Cam jerks back, his eyes full of questions.

But there's no more time for questions. We've wasted far too much of it.

I don't yank his towel off like he did mine. Instead, I lean in to kiss his neck, slowly opening the front knot. With my breath against his warm neck, I place my palm against his most sensitive parts. The towel falls to the floor and he's completely naked, cupped in my hand. I step back, eager to see what's before me.

He's beautiful.

Hung like some god from mythology, he couldn't be any more magnificent. The same Cam, but an entirely different Cam. A man who undeniably wants me. How did I miss this entire chapter of my life, waiting so patiently for me to turn the page?

I pull Cam into a hard kiss, a kiss that says *I'm not letting you go.* He's more than happy to concede to my demands now that his hands have found my bikini-clad ass. He traces the line of fabric before dipping his fingers inside to give me a good squeeze. I gasp, and he smirks against my lips.

I barely notice that he's walking me backward until my knees hit the bed and buckle. I lie back and he moves himself on top of me, dropping needy kisses on my chest that beg for more contact than this bikini will allow. His thick, dark hair is between my fingers, and I can't get enough of the texture. I moan as the corner of his mouth grazes my nipple, just peeking out of its bikini confines. Growing impatient, I pull his face up to mine again, all tongues and love bites.

If I was ever cold from leaving the hot tub, I've forgotten. Hell, I've forgotten what cold even feels like. Here, underneath this man as he moves on top of me, I only feel fire.

There's a pressure against my bikini bottoms. I can feel his need for me, hot and demanding. It's so good, so perfect, and I can't help grinding my hips up against him. *I need you too.*

He makes a low rumbling noise in his throat that causes my stomach to flutter. Dear God, that sound is like music. I've never once heard a noise like that from Cam in my entire life, but suddenly I'm addicted to making him do that again—preferably as soon as freaking possible.

His cock is rubbing perfect circles into my aching clit. God, I could come for him again, just like this.

I reach down, taking his thick length in my hand. A few firm pulls award me the most delicious moan from deep in his throat.

Just think of the sounds he'll make once he's inside me.

I move aside my bikini bottoms, letting him rub his cock all over my wetness. He shudders above me, overtaken with ecstasy.

Still, he hesitates.

I groan and wrap my legs around his hips.

"What do you want?" he whispers.

"You. Inside me." I gasp. "I want you, Cam."

His lips are on mine, hot and demanding, and I cling to him, kissing him back until I'm dizzy.

And just as he begins to press forward against my throbbing flesh, there's a knock at the door.

My stomach clenches as Cam and I both glance toward the sound.

"Hey, let me in."

Fuck.

It's Jack.

CHAPTER Fifteen

Camden

've never hated Jack more than in the moment my dick pressed right up against Natalie's wet center. She shoves me away and I jump back, both of us in a panic. She straightens herself on the rumpled duvet as I yank on a pair of shorts over my obvious erection.

This is bad.

"Dammit, that's Jack," she whispers, her hand over her heart. Her face is pale and her mouth agape. I can tell this will be a situation for me to handle.

Another hammering knock at the door. "Dude, wake up!"

Fuck, fuck, fuck.

"Cool your shit. I'm coming." At least my voice sounds more composed than I feel in this moment.

I tuck my dick into a position that makes my arousal not so obvious and pad over to the door. I look back at Natalie, who is preoccupied with dragging her fingers through her hair. It's in knots, difficult to tame.

I did that.

And I want to do so much more than that. I fight the urge to turn away from the door, grab Natalie by the wrists, and push her back on the bed. I want to drive my dick into her tight heat and pound out every pent-up emotion I've been harboring these past few weeks.

Natalie meets my eyes. Her face turns an even brighter pink. She's still wet, and I know it.

I take a deep breath and open the door.

"Jesus, you sleep like the dead. Oh, hey, Natalie," Jack says, surprise noticeable in his voice. His eyes linger for a moment too long on the rumpled bedspread where Natalie sits as casually as she can in her bikini.

I have no idea if he suspects anything, but if he

does, he doesn't say anything.

"I was just checking on him," Natalie says, her voice a little higher than usual. She's still a bit breathless, and my mouth twitches with the knowledge that I did that to her.

"And what's the diagnosis?" Jack places a hand roughly on my forehead before I smack it off.

"I'm fine. What do you want?"

"We found grape liquor in the bar. Everyone's doing shots like it's fucking junior year and we have finals tomorrow morning. You guys have to come."

Natalie opens her mouth to object, but Jack holds up a hand to silence her.

"Huh-uh. No buts. Hop to it."

Natalie bites her tongue. I can see the tortured look in her eyes, and I can't help but revel in it.

She wants to stay here. She wants to stay here with me.

My heart rate kicks up in my chest. *Don't go . . .* But Natalie quickly snatches her rumpled towel from off the floor as Jack eyes me. After one last lingering look, she lets herself out, the door swinging closed behind her.

I swallow the lump that's formed in my throat, suddenly at a loss for words. The soft sound of her bare feet padding away is the most depressing sound in the entire world.

God fucking dammit. We were so close.

"What's with her?" Jack asks, frowning. I want to punch the stupid look off of his face, but I restrain myself. That's the blue balls talking, not my actual feelings.

"She's fine. But I'm tired as shit, man. Go on without me," I say, steering him toward the door. If I don't take care of this situation in my pants soon, I'm going to be in serious pain for the rest of the night.

I half expect him to pressure me into coming back downstairs, but he must see something in my gaze that assures him that won't be happening.

"When did you become such a party pooper?" he asks as I close the door in his face. "Whatever, man. You're missing out," he calls from the other side of the door.

Fuck yes, I am.

I'm missing out on probably the most incredible opportunity of my life, simply because the timing was shit. What would have happened had Jack not knocked? Would I be fucking Natalie right now? Would I know what her face looks like when I'm inside her? Would I know what her body feels like around mine?

I need another fucking shower.

Ice-cold water hits my shoulders in stinging droplets. My dick remains as hard as an iron rod, erect against my stomach. Still, negative thoughts plague me. What if she never wants to touch me again? What if I scared her away? What if this completely wrecks her trust in me?

I don't even want to jack off. It would be too sad.

Frustrated, I turn off the water and rest my aching head against the cold tile. I don't want to think about what any of this could mean, especially if it means something irreparable has happened between us.

Just breathe.

I'm counting my breaths when I hear a knock at the door. It's barely been twenty minutes since Jack tried to lure me out of my room with the promise of nostalgia. Surely, he doesn't think bringing the party to me will do him any favors.

I rip open the door. "Jack, I said I was—"

It isn't Jack. Natalie stands at the door. The first thing I notice is that her hair is up in a messy pony-tail, the tangled waves falling from the top of her head to the nape of her neck. Her towel is gone, and she's just standing there at my door in her skimpy bikini. I can see her nipples through the damp fabric of her lavender bathing suit. The pale hair on her arms stands on end. Her eyes are searching mine.

"Natalie."

She reaches up and covers my mouth with her fingers, walking me backward into my room. With her other hand, she reaches up and pulls me down to her level. The door clicks shut softly behind us.

What?

Natalie kisses me. Her lips pull and push against mine, her tongue prodding my mouth in a desperate exploration. She tastes like grape liquor.

I pull back. "What are you doing?"

"Kissing you," she says, her eyes hooded, her gaze fixed on my mouth.

"What about everyone else?"

"They're drunk. They'll be in bed soon. It's just us."

It's just us.

Us.

I yank her body against me, her bare stomach pressing intimately into mine. She's so soft and smooth, and the feel of her against me immediately short-circuits everything else.

Us.

I take her ponytail in my hand and move her head to the side to give my tongue better access. She bites me then, nibbling my lower lip, and I groan, pressing her hard into the door. I'm holding her wrists against the door, nipping and sucking at the long line of her neck. She pulls my pelvis into hers with a leg curved around my waist, rubbing my cock into her.

Fuck. It feels incredible.

She moans, her lips parting. I can't help it. I place a finger into her mouth, just to feel her tongue. Just to imagine.

She sucks hard on my finger, her eyes blazing pure fire into mine. I drop to my knees before her, pressing needy kisses into her belly, relishing the silky skin there. I don't need to ask what she wants. *Where* she wants me. I can feel it in the way she drags her nails against my scalp, pushing my head lower and lower. With hooked fingers, I drag her itsy bikini bottoms down. Her plump, eager pussy greets me. It's more beautiful than I remember. I drag my teeth across the tender flesh of her thigh, lifting it over my shoulder. She's whimpering, barely able to stand.

"Please, Cam, please . . ."

The sound of my name falling from her lips so lustfully has me hungry to taste her. I wrap my arm around her thigh and press my lips firmly against her throbbing clit. She gasps, her knees buckling. With my other hand, I brace her, my fingers tucked tightly against the firm muscles of her ass. Her fingers pull at my hair, a silent invitation for *more*.

Oh, I'll give you more.

I trace her clit with my tongue in soft, teasing circles. With each flick, she melts against me, her fingers pulling at my hair. With each suck, her sexy moans grow louder and louder.

"Shh," I whisper, my lips never abandoning her sweet pussy. "Someone will hear us."

She covers her own mouth with a hand, her eyes closed. From this angle, I can look up at her, watch her breasts bounce with every unrelenting rock against my mouth. I can see her try to stifle every whimper, and fail. It only makes me suck her clit harder.

I increase my pace. I want her to fall apart against my tongue. I have to see her lose all control. Her hips are bucking against me in a wild dance. I can feel her whole body jerk as she comes, her opening tightening and trembling. She cries out with deep, gulping breaths.

So beautiful.

I could stay like this forever, licking her, teasing her.

But Natalie is impatient.

"Get up here," she gasps.

Her eyes are dark with lust, her cheeks bright spots of pink as she watches me. I'm more turned on than I've ever been in my entire life, and my heart is jackhammering against my rib cage.

I stand, touching one finger to my lips, which are still damp from her orgasm. "You taste so fucking good." My voice is deep and husky.

Natalie touches my bare chest, her palm resting flat against my pec muscle.

"You came back." I smile, loving the feel of her hand on me, no matter how innocent the touch.

She smiles and wraps her arms around me, pulling me against her heaving chest. Her lips press against my throat, eliciting a shuddering breath from me. Her hands trail up and down my back, her fingers finding purchase in my ass. Before long, the towel around my waist is in a damp pile at our feet and Natalie's hand is rubbing up and down my cock.

Jesus.

We're right back where we were before, frantically touching each other, walking back to my hotel bed. This time, it's my knees that hit the edge of the bed, forcing me to sit before her, my cock bouncing heavily against my stomach. She uses both of her small hands to wrap around its girth, pulling me up and down.

Holy shit.

I feel my desire growing in the base of my dick, a soft tingling warmth with promises of a hefty release. I lean back on my hands, watching as Natalie jerks me off, her gaze locked on my cock like it's the most exquisite piece of art she's ever laid eyes on. I'm bubbling over, pre-come dripping down the side of my dick.

She licks her lips.

No fucking way.

Natalie's little pink tongue peeks out of her mouth. She catches the drop with her tongue, licking all the way up to the head.

I might pass out.

I could die now and be a happy man.

My best friend's mouth is on my dick, and this should be weird, but instead it's the best thing I've ever experienced.

"Fuck, Natalie." I touch her cheek, stroking the soft skin there. "It's so good. So fucking good."

That affirmation appears to be all it takes for Natalie to take me deep into her mouth. Natalie. Sweet, clueless, gorgeous Natalie isn't shy at all with my dick bobbing against her tongue. She adds one hand, gripping me low on the shaft as her tongue does the most magical things to my cock.

"Yes, oh fuck." I groan again.

She takes me deep, gulping me in, letting me pop back out, sucking me right back in. There has never been a more satisfying feeling than the hot, wet slide of this woman's mouth around my pulsing dick.

"Come for me," she whispers before taking me in deep again, her ponytail bouncing with her increased efforts.

Yes, ma'am.

When I can't take it any longer, I let go. The hot, searing come shoots out of me, straight into the back of her throat, where she gulps me down. She takes each spurt with a diligent swallow until I'm dizzy.

Completely sated, I fall back onto my elbows, my arms shaking and chest heaving. This woman has made me orgasm faster, harder, than any woman in my life ever has. I can't even catch my breath with her little tongue licking soft lines up my cock, cleaning it for me.

So fucking hot.

My turn again.

I yank Natalie up onto the bed. She topples next to me with a loud laugh. Is that my favorite sound? That unabashed sound of joy she saves just for me?

Or is it that shameless cry she makes when she comes apart at my command?

I guess there's only one way to find out.

"Again?" she asks breathlessly as my fingers trace her lower lip.

I press my mouth to hers in another searing kiss.

Right now, there's no thoughts of Jack or if our friends suspect anything, or how this might irreparably change our friendship. Right now there's only heat and lust and our two bodies grinding closer as we recline onto the bed together.

I push the tip of my finger inside her tight heat to answer that ridiculous question. She closes her eyes, her eyelashes casting dark shadows onto her cheeks. As my finger begins a steady pumping rhythm inside her, Natalie's head falls back onto the covers and she hums with desire.

Yes, you beautiful woman. Again.

CHAPTER
Sixteen

Natalie

I sigh. My queen-size hotel bed is painfully empty with just me under its covers. I splay my arms and legs as wide as I can, but I still don't cover the whole bed. It's three in the morning, and I've been trying to sleep for over an hour. My thoughts refuse to quiet the hell down. I've been replaying the night over and over in my mind, retracing every caress, every goose bump. It was . . . earth shattering.

Everything I thought I knew about Cam is now magnified under an entirely new lens. His sexy little smile, the way my name sounds when he whispers it in a rough growl against my mouth. What he tastes like. Jesus, how hung he is. It's all so foreign to me, and I can't wait to investigate further.

Further.

Will we go further? We've already done more than I've ever imagined, but what would be next? Is there even a next time? What if this was a one-time deal between very, *very* good friends? What if he was just horny, and I was lucky enough to be in the right place at the right time?

I'm gonna make myself sick with these spiraling questions. I've never been comfortable with the unknown. Whenever there's an issue between the guys and me, I just address it directly. That's right. The answers are out there . . . I just need to ask for them.

I reach under my pillow and pull out my cell phone, typing out a message before I can second-guess myself.

Are you asleep?

My cell phone falls to my chest with a hollow thud. I chew on a nail. If he doesn't respond tonight, I'm going to gnaw my whole arm off. Or at least lose a night's sleep.

Buzz, buzz.

Yeah.

Thank God.

Smartass.

I smile. This level of rapport will never be damaged, no matter how many times we get each other off.

Are you okay?

Shit. I guess it does look suspicious that I'm awake at three in the morning. Still, for all he knows, I could just be asking for a late-night movie recommendation. Yet, I feel the weight of those three words, as heavy as the barbells I lift at the gym. How does he always know exactly how I'm feeling, every time? My heart aches.

I'm okay, just confused.

About earlier?

Yeah. What does it mean?

My heart is beating fast in my ears. God, what a girlie thing to ask. It was probably just a one-time hookup. It probably meant nothing, means nothing. And now I can't tell if I'm excited for his response or dreading it. Knowing my propensity for mixed emotions, it's both.

It doesn't have to mean any-thing. It felt good for both of us, right?

Good is a glaring understatement.

Yeah, it did. I guess you're right.

Get some sleep, Nat.

Night, Cam.

I toss my phone aside, and it bounces pathetically on this horrid hotel mattress. It's fine, I know it's fine. I pull the covers tightly under my chin and turn over to sleep. Cam is right. It was really good, and that's great, and nothing has to change. We've snapped right back to normal, and that's exactly what I wanted.

Then what's this ache in my chest about?

• • •

Janelle attacks me with a bear hug as soon as I walk out of my supervisor's office one day the next week. I've just finished the meeting I've been waiting ages for. The promotion: Will she or won't she?

"What did I say?" she cries, rocking me back and forth.

"I got the promotion. You were right!" I enjoy the embrace for as long as I can, knowing my own mother isn't as proud of me as this woman right here in my arms. Once again, I'm reminded of how good I've got it here.

I am now the newest member of the management team, overseeing digital marketing for this little nonprofit that's come to feel like home.

"Are you going to celebrate that new paycheck?"

"Of course!"

"With your boyfriend?" She waggles her thin eyebrows at me.

"No such boyfriend anymore," I confess. "But I have some pretty great friends to share the moment with."

Cam is the one who pops into my head first, though.

"A good friend goes much further than any boyfriend. Lemme tell you that," Janelle says in a low, sage voice, as if she's revealing some age-old wisdom.

She's right. I'm absolutely beaming. I can't wait to tell the guys.

"You have fun tonight, honey!"

As Janelle walks away, I pull out my phone, drafting the message.

Hear ye, hear ye! Your girl has
finally acquired the fabled pro-

motion! Drinks tonight on me??

My thumb hesitates over the SEND button. Apparently, muscle memory isn't more powerful than my fear of confronting Cam. It's been a few days since that night at the hotel. If I don't see him now, will I keep avoiding him forever? That seems unlikely. Jack certainly wouldn't allow that to happen. I can be a big girl and keep my libido in check. Still, I feel a blush creeping up my cheeks.

Whatever. You deserve this.

And who better to celebrate this milestone with than my two best friends?

I hit SEND and let the celebrating commence.

• • •

Even the way Cam's lips wrap around a damn sushi roll has me thinking dirty thoughts. The line of his jaw clenching and unclenching hurtles me back down memory lane. You know, the memory with my mouth on his cock.

After a little dispute on the proper cuisine for such an occasion, we've landed at my favorite sushi bar downtown. Both the guys are shoveling down spicy tuna, but I barely have an appetite for the cottage-cheese-and-avocado roll on my plate. I push it around restlessly, as if the smears of soy sauce would somehow reveal my future.

Our future, more precisely.

"Hey, Moore," Jack says through a mouthful of rice. "Why the focus-face?"

I laugh halfheartedly. I'm not focused at all. I'm barely present. How am I supposed to focus on anything when all I can think about is kissing Cam?

"Just thinking about work."

"What does this promotion mean for you?" Cam asks. Even his voice makes me tingly. *Dammit.*

"It means I get to make more of the marketing decisions, larger scale. What promotions or events to advertise, when, where, and how. I get to develop the whole marketing strategy. It's what I've wanted since I was hired."

"She's power hungry," Jack whispers to Cam. Cam's perfect lips curl into a sexy smirk as he glances at me. I avert my gaze immediately.

Well, that was subtle.

I can feel Cam's inquisitive gaze on me as Jack continues to fictionalize my rise to power and prestige in the nonprofit sector. Cam's most definitely aware of my strange behavior. I can't help it. If I look him in the eyes too long, I'm afraid I'll melt into a puddle of lust-struck goo. I stare purposely at Jack but don't hear a word he says.

"And with that, I say we make a toast," Jack finishes. He lifts his sake to eye level, and Cam and I follow suit.

"To the best friend neither of us deserves. Natalie, you're the best friend two dudes could ask for. To the many years ahead of us!"

"Cheers," Cam adds with a brilliant smile.

My eyes are smarting with fresh tears, but I manage to clink my sake with theirs. It's *me* who doesn't deserve *them*. How could I, while I'm lusting after the taller, sexier friend?

I need to get a grip, and get it fast. If I don't, I may lose both of these incredible men forever.

Is this desire between Cam and me stronger than the desire to maintain the friendship between the two of them?

Suddenly, I hope not.

.

CHAPTER
Seventeen

Camden

"I hate tuxes," Jack grumbles, tugging at the collar of his shirt.

"You look good," I reply. We're in Natalie's childhood bedroom, adjusting our tuxes in the small vanity mirror. The rest of the bridal party is scattered throughout the upstairs bedrooms, doing the same. Natalie, ever the giver in our group of friends, recognized how expensive the resort was going to be for Jessie and Tyron to book at the last minute. She offered her family's mansion for the wedding ceremony and reception since they wanted to get married right away—before Tyron deploys again.

"My parents won't mind," she assured Tyron and Jessie. "They're out of the country. They'll be more bummed that they're going to miss it."

Jack shifts uncomfortably in his formal wear. Personally, I love a good tuxedo. I don't get the opportunity to look this nice very often. And as far as I'm concerned, a wedding is a perfect chance to dig it out of my closet.

"You look like James Bond," Jack complains. "I look like a fucking penguin."

"A handsome lady-killer penguin," I say, straightening his bow tie for him with a smirk.

Jack swats my hands away and plops down with a loud groan on Natalie's bed. The room is nothing like her. The walls are stripes of white and black, stark and modern. Nothing like the sweet, soft Natalie that I know. The only thing that reminds me of her is the knitted blanket at the end of her bed. I'm sure she made it herself.

"Speaking of ladies," Jack says, cutting into my thoughts. "I don't know how much longer I can hold off."

"What do you mean?"

"On the bet. We're at a wedding. What are weddings for?"

"The union of two people in love?"

"What? Nooo. Hooking up with bridesmaids. It's like I don't even know you." Jack shakes his head in disgust. I chuckle. Little does he know; he's already won that bet. I'm not about to tell him that I've been fooling around with our best friend behind his back.

Maybe not ever.

"Tomorrow's the thirty-day mark and we'll be off the hook," I point out.

"Yeah, and I barely fucking made it through. Damn dick's practically been rubbed raw."

There's a knock at the door.

"Yoo-hoo, coming in." Natalie peeks her head in, her hair falling off her shoulder in loosely styled waves. Her makeup is natural, accentuating the angles and curves of her face. She's beautiful, of course.

"Shit, you guys look great." She frowns dramatically.

"Why the face?" Jack asks.

"Because I have to wear this." Natalie opens

the door the rest of the way, allowing us to fully take in the disaster before us.

"It's orange," I say.

"*Tangerine*, to be precise," she says with finger quotes. "Jessie's favorite color. So here I am."

"You look more like a pumpkin," Jack says with a laugh, and she flips him off.

"And there's no one better to pull off that look." I watch her try to fight a small smile, but it curls up the corners of her mouth. Small victories.

"Well, Jack, you'd better find Meredith. She's gonna be pissed if she has to keep looking for you," Natalie says, shooing him out the door.

"Here I go." Jack sighs. He sulks out of the room with a halfhearted salute.

Jack closes the door behind us, and it's just Natalie and me in the room now. Just Natalie and me in the entire world.

God, I want to tell her how beautiful she is.

"No date to the wedding?" I ask, my voice tight.

"No." She scoffs. "Who would I ask?"

"You could have your pick of any men."

"And you could have your pick of any women. But you're alone today too."

There are words hanging between us, words neither of us will say. The memory of what we did in that hotel bed is so fresh, I can almost still taste her kisses. Part of me is relieved we didn't go any further. If I knew what it was like to be inside her, I know I'd have a hard time keeping my cool around her. I don't have a witty response to her statement, just a silent acknowledgment that we're both here alone, and neither of us knows what to do about it.

"Ready?" she asks.

"Of course." I offer her my arm. It takes her a moment, but Natalie accepts it. She loops her hand through my arm, and together, we join our friends.

Over the course of the evening, we all get a lot drunker faster than any of us expect. Natalie's parents have an excessive amount of alcohol in their home, and we certainly have helped ourselves. It was a small ceremony, just a handful of friends and family. But it was beautiful. I couldn't help but look over at Natalie as Tyron and Jessie were exchanging their original vows. But she wasn't looking at the couple.

Was she looking at me?

I didn't have time to dwell too much on that possibility as the groom kissed the bride and the dancing commenced. It takes a lot of alcohol to get me on a dance floor, and Jack and Natalie weren't going to let me spend the night sober, sitting on the sidelines.

Here I am now, reasonably drunk, my bow tie hanging loosely from my neck. We're all eating wedding cake while watching the bride and groom dance the final song, wrapped in each other's arms. They're a picture of perfect love and commitment. And if I were to think about it enough, they're the picture of the same things that I want with Natalie, but I can't let my mind go there for even a moment.

"Isn't it beautiful?" Natalie asks me as the song reaches a close, interrupting my melancholy thoughts. There are tears in her eyes.

"Yeah," I say, my eyes never leaving her face. I don't care if she never loves me. I will always look at her like this.

"Why are you staring at me?"

I reach over to her and wipe a small fleck of white frosting from her lip. When I lick it off my thumb, her face grows pink, and I smile. Maybe it's not hopeless after all, but this is neither the time nor the place to showcase any feelings we might have for each other. We both know lines were drawn and lines were crossed, and now we're operating in a gray area. I want to hold her, want to say a thousand things to her, but instead, I just stand there quietly.

About an hour later, a limo arrives to whisk the happy couple away. As the guests begin to say their good-byes and trickle out, I pour myself another glass.

Before long, Jack and I are sitting on the steps of the foyer's grand staircase, our jackets hanging over chairs in the other room. Jack's arm drapes loosely around my shoulders.

"I have a confession to make," he says, slurring his words.

"Uh-oh."

"I'm going to lose this bet." He snickers.

"Why's that?"

"Meredith definitely wants me."

We exchange a look and crack up at this turn of events.

"Do you want her?"

"Fuck if I know! My dick hasn't had any action from anything other than my hand the past month. I'm not sure if I still know what to do. Wish me luck!" He plants a sloppy, drunken kiss on my cheek and stumbles away. I would chase after him, but the guy deserves a little excitement after this month of celibacy. I'm glad he's finally feeling up to the chase again. I watch in amusement as he offers to share a cab ride home with Meredith, and she grins and accepts.

The place is trashed. While most guests took a centerpiece of flowers home with them, they left behind their dinner remnants and half-empty glasses.

Where is Natalie? I know her parents usually employ a cleaning crew, but that doesn't seem like her style. I can imagine it now. "I have two perfectly good hands," she would say.

I roll my eyes, then decide another pair of hands

would make this process a lot easier and faster. I rummage around in the cabinets for a trash bag, and then begin my trek across the large expanse of the Moore mansion. First, the banquet hall.

As I squat down to pick up a bit of cake that must have jumped ship, I hear footsteps and turn to see Natalie walking down the stairs.

"Good-bye!" she calls to some unknown guests as they leave. The door clicks shut, and the house is silent. Natalie stands there alone on the staircase landing, perfectly still.

What is she thinking about?

She must shake off whatever feeling is holding her there, because she heads down the stairs. She holds up the hem of the tangerine dress in her hands, careful not to drag it on the floor. She hates the thing, but still takes care of it.

Classic Natalie.

I should tell her I'm still here so I don't frighten her. But I keep my mouth shut.

Natalie walks up to the remaining pile of cake still sitting on the elaborately decorated cart. With a finger, she swipes a dollop of frosting and brings it to her mouth. She doesn't eat it quite yet, however. First, she presses the frosting lightly against her lips and closes her eyes. I'm mesmerized.

Now, really. What the hell is she thinking about?

After a moment, she dips her finger into her mouth, tasting the vanilla fluff. I watch as her eyelids flutter, and imagine she's overcome with the sweet, savory taste on her finger.

When I rise to my feet, Natalie jumps, her hand over her heart.

"Oh my God, Cam! You fucking scared me."

"Sorry. How's the cake?"

She blushes. "What are you still doing here?"

"I thought I would help you clean up." I lift the trash bag in explanation and she looks away, almost abruptly. *Is she annoyed? What's wrong?*

"You really don't have to do that. My parents already called the cleaning staff to take care of it all in the morning. I told them I'd do it myself, but . . ." She trails off, shrugging. "They never listen."

I close the distance between us, walking across the parquet floor to meet her. There's only a foot of air between us now.

"I'll listen. Tell me where to start." I could kick myself for seeming too eager. Natalie meets my eyes reluctantly as a smile curls her lips. I don't mind so much making a fool of myself if this is my reward.

"My hero. It's really not necessary. Thank you, though," she says softly, reaching out to place her hand on my arm. I can feel her touch burn through my dress shirt.

"In that case, would you like to share a cab home?"

She rubs her thumb against my arm, a familiar and exciting feeling. Is she doing that on purpose? She doesn't seem to be aware, as if it's merely a reflex of our bodies being so close.

"I thought I'd just stay here tonight."

"Of course."

Her eyes search my face. What is she looking for? What can I give her?

I just want to kiss her. I want to press her against me, rake my fingers through her hair, feel her breath on my lips.

"I'll take that," she murmurs. She drops her hand from my arm to my hand, where I hold the trash bag. Her fingers brush mine and halt. I can hear my own heart pounding a passionate rhythm in my chest.

Instinctively, I pull her fingers into my palm, letting the trash bag fall to the floor.

We both watch our hands twine with each other to form an intricate knot that neither of us intended. It's our bodies, instinctively having their way with each other. I can't stop my thumb from rubbing circles into her knuckles, desperate for the contact. She squeezes back.

If she isn't going to stop, neither am I.

"Natalie."

She looks up at me, her lips parted, her eyes wide. I can tell by the rise and fall of her chest how hard it is for her to breathe.

I feel the same way.

"Cam—"

I kiss her softly on the lips, the lightest of

touches. I step closer to press my lips a fraction more firmly against hers, letting my eyes drift shut.

There are only two points of connection. Our intertwined hands and our lips. She stays like that, frozen and still, until my mouth breaks from hers. I open my eyes, daring her. *Go ahead. Deny this.*

Her eyes sparkle in the dim light as she shakes her head, ever so slightly. Then she reaches up so, so slowly. The back of her fingers brush against my jawline before she places her warm palm against my cheek. Her lips curl up.

Does that mean—

She answers my unspoken question with her mouth on mine. I suck in a breath. I thought kissing Natalie was the best feeling. No, the best feeling is being kissed *by* Natalie. Our kisses, once so fragile and tentative, become hard and wanting. She gasps against my mouth as I hold her waist, pulling her flush against my body.

I want you. So fucking badly.

These words fill my mind, threatening to spill out of my mouth. When they do, Natalie moans against me, drawing herself up on her toes.

"I want you too," she whispers back.

It's a blur of hands, lips, and whispers then. Before I know it, I've hoisted Natalie up. Her legs are around my hips and she grinds against me. I'm hard in an instant, which makes it difficult to walk, but I manage. We stumble up the stairs—me half carrying her, and her dragging me with her. It's not the most graceful thing, but neither of us seems to care. We're laughing and kissing and apologizing. It's just so very us.

Once we reach her bedroom, I kick open the door, shuffling backward into the darkness. She slides down from my arms, shoving me onto the bed. I land with a bounce, the wind knocked out of me. But she gives me no time to recover before she climbs on top of me.

All I can do is hold on as she kisses me hard on the mouth while she rubs herself against my pelvis. I'm hard in the way I'm only hard for this woman in my arms. She tears at the buttons of my shirt, exposing my chest to her curious lips and tongue. It feels so insanely good to know that she wants me as much as I want her. I fumble with her hideous dress, trying to find the zipper or the buttons or whatever will get this orange monstrosity off of her. She laughs breathlessly into my ear.

"It's on the side, you dope," she whispers. I find the zipper and pull, desperate to feel her breasts in my hands again. It catches on the scratchy fabric, refusing to budge.

"Fuck this dress." I growl out the words, and with both hands, I rip the fabric where the zipper snags. Natalie giggles as I flip her over to nibble on her exposed neck and chest. Laughter turns to sighs as I rediscover all of her most sensitive spots along her throat and collarbone. I graze my teeth against her skin, and her hips buck up to meet mine.

Fuck, Cam. Take it slow.

I tell myself this, but my fingers still find her thigh, gliding upward to her hot, wet center. I tease her, using one fingertip to draw an inquisitive line along her panties. She squirms against my hand and bites my shoulder. Hard.

"Ow." I snicker.

"Don't tease," she says with a pout, and I smirk.

"You don't like that?" I rub her right where she needs it. She clenches her jaw and closes her eyes. I haven't moved aside the fabric yet, but I can feel how wet she already is.

"Please, Cam," she whimpers. I pull at her dress with my teeth, and when I rub my nose against her nipple, she gasps. "Please, what?"

"Touch me."

Anything for you.

I push one finger into her then, eliciting a strangled cry from her. I tease her, savoring each little sound that escapes her. She reaches down, fumbling for my zipper. It takes her far less time than it took me to figure it out. In seconds, she has my engorged length in her hand.

This is going so fast. Too fast.

Three seconds later, I finally have her out of that damn dress, and my pants and boxers are shoved down. Settling in my lap, Natalie rubs the tip of my cock against her silken wet core, egging me on.

Fuck.

"I don't have a condom with me," I groan through gritted teeth.

"What, you didn't think we were going to be

doing this tonight?" She smirks, her cheeks painted red. She may sound cocky, but I know she's just as in awe of this as I am. I dip my head down and flick her erect nipple with my tongue. She shivers.

"A man can dream."

"Hold on."

Natalie props herself up on her elbows, giving herself enough leverage to reach over and rifle through the top drawer of her nightstand. Then, this beautiful creature with her mussed hair and half-torn dress pulls an entire roll of new condoms out of the drawer. Is this a goddamn magic trick or am I actually this lucky?

She grins sheepishly at me. "What?"

"You're perfect."

"Don't you want to know why I have these? My mom thought I was too much of a prude, so she gave—"

"I don't care," I mutter against her lips, crushing them with a kiss. I rip a single condom off the roll, leaning back to slide it on.

"Let me," she says, her eyes wide and eager.

She takes the condom from my hand, slowly guiding it along my length. She breathes her warmth against my neck while her hands stroke against my shielded cock. I shudder. This is excruciatingly magnificent.

When Natalie lies down next to me, I move over top of her, our chests touching skin to skin.

"You sure?" I ask.

"Yeah," she whispers.

I nod. With one long, slow thrust, I push inside the hottest, tightest heat I've ever felt. Natalie cries out.

"Are you okay?"

"Yes, fuck. Yes . . ." She gasps. "Just more."

And I give her exactly that.

Jesus.

Natalie fits me better than I could have ever imagined. And I did imagine. This is every fantasy I've had for the past few weeks, now come to life. And it's better than any dream I've ever had.

Shit.

I'm going to lose my shit soon if I don't take it slow. I need to relish the embrace of her arms, her lips, her pussy. I can't take any of this for granted, because this very well may not ever happen again with the obstacles we both have to face.

The question is, how much longer can I last?

CHAPTER
Eighteen

Natalie

I was right. The sounds Cam makes while he's inside me are more satisfying than any fine wine.

"Fuck, Natalie, you're perfect."

These short, breathy words rush into me, filling me. With each deep, meaningful thrust, I float even higher.

Cam's lips trace my collarbone as his deft fingers rub tight circles against my clit. His thrusts are shallow, teasing me with promises of even more pleasure. But I'm greedy as all hell.

"Cam!" I gasp. "Please!"

He dips his arm beneath one of my legs, shifting his angle of penetration. With a slow, patient thrust, he finally fills me to the hilt. His pelvic bone is flush against my clit, pressing unforgiving pressure against that needy bundle of nerves. I buck unconsciously, my back arching.

One of his hands slips behind me to support my writhing body. The other gathers my hair at the base of my neck and pulls, revealing a sensitive spot of my neck and angling my aching breasts toward the ceiling. Never one to leave me wanting, he draws my painfully erect nipple into his mouth. His tongue flicks and teases it. I cry out, losing my mind with the feeling. Soon, his tongue lathing my breasts synchronizes with his hip thrusting as he pushes himself deep into my body, which is suddenly so needy for him.

How is he so good at this?

Each roll of sensation shoots shivers from my nipple to my clit and back again. I can feel him growling against my sternum, losing some of his perfect control.

"God, I've wanted to feel you . . ."

"How long?"

"Forever."

His mouth is on my throat, and I'm seeing stars.

"Oh, Cam," I cry, suddenly so, so close.

"Is it good?" he whispers against the column of my throat, and I dig my fingers into his muscled ass, pulling him even deeper.

His thick length hits me in just the right spot, and we both feel it. That explosive connection that's about to combust.

He fits me like he was always meant to.

"Yes, yes, yes . . ." I can't stop the word from slipping out of my lips. I'm quickly arriving at a place I've never been before. Suddenly, I'm terrified that I won't ever recover from this, this blinding pleasure, and that no one else will ever again measure up.

I don't have time to think any more as pleasure pulses through me. My walls clench and unclench around Cam's impressive girth. He's perfect. It's like he was made for me.

My cry of ecstasy is muffled by his kiss, tongue against tongue. Shivering with pleasure, I come undone around him. He pumps faster, gaining just enough traction to then lose himself. Cam groans into my mouth, matching me shudder for shudder.

His body drapes across mine in an embrace of hot skin. I cling to him, refusing to let this perfect moment end just yet. Our bodies are still sensitive with the aftershocks of that sexual earthquake.

Laughter bubbles out of me before I realize what is funny.

"What?" Cam asks, his lips moving pleasantly against my collarbone.

"We're so stupid."

"Why's that?"

"We could have been fucking for the past decade," I say between gulps of air. My heart is still pounding.

He chuckles. "You wouldn't have wanted to have sex with me back in high school."

"And why's that?"

"I didn't know any tricks yet," he whispers, drawing a featherlight circle around my nipple. It perks up without my permission.

"No fair." I pout, rubbing my leg against his

upper thigh. Even the lightest of touches wakes up his cock. I feel it hardening again against my hip.

"Hey now," Cam says, propping his head against a free hand. The flush of his cheeks and the smile on his face make me so happy.

"Hey now," I repeat, pressing one hand to his scruffy jaw so I can draw him in for a soft, warm kiss. He wraps his arms around me, pulling me against him as we settle under the sheets.

All the time I spent sleeping in a bed alone, I had no idea what I was missing. I knew I was lonely, but not to this extent. My heart aches.

"What's wrong?" he asks, always knowing.

"Nothing. I'm just happy."

With that, he squeezes me tighter. There's no place I'd rather be than here, dozing off in my best friend's embrace.

• • •

"What the fuck?"

My eyes snap open. Cam jolts up beside me, yanking the sheet over my naked chest. It takes me a moment to know what startled him.

Jack.

He's standing there with rubber gloves and a garbage bag slung over his shoulder.

"Jack!" I squeak. "What are you doing here?"

"I came to help clean up," he says. His voice is empty and cold. Cam grabs hold of a pillow, tossing it over his waist as he gets out of bed. "Look, Jack—"

But Jack doesn't stick around long enough to hear Cam's explanation. He turns and hauls ass out of the room, and I hear a door slam distantly a few moments later. My throat goes completely dry, and I feel faint.

"Shit," Cam says under his breath. I hear my pulse, a frantic drum in my ears. I can't breathe.

"Nat?"

Cam's voice is distant and garbled. My stomach churns, like I might throw up. His hands on my cheeks pull me back into the moment.

"Nat, just breathe."

"Cam— Cam!" I gasp.

"You're okay. It's going to be fine. Just breathe."

Nothing is fine.

Jack has been one of my very best friends for over a decade. And now I've betrayed him.

"What does he think? Is he angry? He seemed so upset. Oh my God, what are we going to do?" Tears slip from my eyes, burning trails down my cheeks and Cam's fingers.

"You didn't do anything wrong. We didn't do anything wrong." Cam wraps me in his arms, and I pull in shuddering breaths against his warm chest. He feels so strong and solid, but inside, I feel like my entire world is crumbling.

I knew that the threat of losing one of my best friends would hurt, but I didn't think it would *break* me like this. And I never thought it would be *Jack.*

"It's my fault," Cam murmurs. "I'm going to fix it."

The space he filled in my bed is suddenly very empty. He's up, pushing his limbs through last night's clothes.

"It's gonna be okay," he promises. He drops a kiss on my head before he walks out the door. Downstairs, the front door clicks shut behind him.

I scrub the tears from my eyes, but my hands still shake.

What was I thinking?

How could we have been so stupid?

The most incredible night of my life might become the biggest mistake of my life. We were selfish. We should have known that this would change our friendship with Jack, or even ruin it.

But then something even more terrifying than that occurs to me. Did I just ruin my friendship with Cam too?

CHAPTER
Nineteen

Camden

What the fuck was I thinking?

My stomach churns as I make the short drive back to the apartment I share with Jack. It's not the effects of the alcohol I drank last night making me feel sick. It's the way his face contorted when he saw Natalie and me in bed together.

Gripping the steering wheel tighter, I step on the gas. I knew what I was doing was wrong, sneaking around behind my best friend's back with the one girl we always swore was off-limits, but every time I was with Natalie, none of that mattered to me. It was worth the risk. *She* was worth the risk. Now, though? After seeing the hurt and confusion in Jack's expression—yeah, I feel like the world's biggest asshole.

This isn't me. I don't sneak around and fuck over my friends. I'm a grown-ass man, and I should have behaved like one. I should have sat him down and come clean about how I was feeling. Maybe he would have understood and given me his blessing, and then again, maybe he wouldn't have. What would I have done then? Because I'm pretty sure not pursuing Natalie isn't an option.

My feelings have grown so much that, honestly, I don't think I could go back to being just friends. Even after today, if that's what they both want, I don't see it being possible. And the thought of that is fucking torture. The idea of walking away from half a lifetime's worth of rock-solid friendship because I couldn't keep my dick in my pants? I groan and slam my fist against the steering wheel.

Finally, I turn onto our street and park my car. Then I jog up to our apartment and burst inside.

"Jack?" I shuffle back to his bedroom when I don't find him in the living room. He's not here.

Seconds later, I'm back out the door, headed to the only other place I think he might be—the bar.

It's only eight in the morning, but when I stroll in, he's already here. Jack is crouched behind the bar, the sound of bottles clinking together as he works.

"Hey." He greets me without turning, his voice flat.

"Hey." I take a tentative step closer. Jack doesn't turn to face me, and honestly, I'm not sure I could handle seeing his wounded expression any-way. He has every right to deck me, to scream and curse and tell me to get the fuck out, but instead he continues stocking the bottles of beer inside the cooler beneath the bar. Somehow, that makes ev-erything ten thousand times worse.

Running my hands along the worn surface of the bar, I inhale deeply, steeling my nerves and try-ing to figure out what the fuck I'm going to say. A million options flash through my head, but none of them seem adequate, and a simple *I'm sorry* won't work at all. Because deep down, I'm not sorry. Be-ing with Natalie was everything.

"So . . ." I drum my thumbs along the cool sur-face of the bar until Jack finally stops and turns around.

"Why didn't you just fucking tell me?"

My throat goes dry. God, I feel like a fucking asshole. Scrubbing my hands through my already messy hair, I release a deep breath. "And say what? That I'm in love with her?"

His eyes meet mine, and they're so dark, so angry. It's so unlike Jack that my stomach tightens.

"It's about damn time you realized it."

The fuck? "You knew?"

He snorts, then rolls his eyes. "Everyone knew except for the two of you. Why do you think I took that stupid bet with you? Why do you think I introduced her to Ben?"

Jack's words are like a shock to my system. It takes me almost a full minute to respond. None of this makes any sense. He knew? The entire fucking time?

"To get me to get my head out of my ass?" I ask.

This can't be. I lean against the bar, suddenly needing more support.

"Yes, basically," he says.

Sinking down onto a bar stool, I push my hands through my hair. "Sorry. I'm just a little fucking confused right now."

Jack smirks. "So . . . was last night the first time?"

I grin crookedly. I can't believe he's asking me that. There's also no way I'm telling him. "Maybe."

The smile spreading across my face against my will tells him everything he needs to know.

I let out a short bark of laughter. "God, I'm so relieved, man. I thought you were ready to punch me in the face."

He shrugs. "Nah. I knew how you feel about her. It's pretty obvious. I know you pretty well, dude."

"True."

"But . . ." He pauses, looking me straight in the eye. "If you hurt her, I will hunt you down and skin you alive."

"That's fair. I definitely don't plan on ever hurting her."

Jack nods, and I can see some uncertainty pass

through his gaze. "I don't know what happens next, that's for you two to figure out, but just promise me one thing."

"Anything." Well, not anything. If he asks me to stop seeing her, that's not something I can promise. I can't just turn off these feelings I have for her. They've been building for thirteen years.

"Promise me that our friendship won't change." He holds out his hand, and I give it a shake.

"Deal."

Then Jack grins at me. "Now, what the fuck are you doing here? Go get your girl."

• • •

Hours later, I still haven't found Natalie. She didn't answer the phone when I called, so I wasn't sure where she might be. Trusting my gut instinct, figuring she wouldn't be at her family's mansion any longer than necessary, I went to her condo, but there was no answer. So I went to her parents' house, but she wasn't there either. Then I headed to the lake spot we used to go to in high school, figuring maybe she went there to think, but no one was there. After going home to shower and change into fresh clothes, now I'm back at her condo, and there's still no sign of her.

Fuck.

Where are you, Nat?

I sink onto the floor outside her front door and lean my head back against the wall. I'm exhausted from getting very little sleep last night, and from all the uncertainty swimming in my gut. My eyes fall closed and I take a deep breath. It's all I can do at the moment, so I focus on taking one deep breath in, and then out.

• • •

"Cam?" Natalie's voice rouses me awake. I blink up at her, realizing it's twilight outside now. "I guess I must have dozed off."

"What are you doing here?" Frowning down at me, she shoves her key into the lock and opens the door.

"Thought we needed to talk," I say, rising to my feet.

"Yeah, I guess we do. Come inside?"

I follow her in, that same uneasy feeling settling low in my gut. Her expression is unreadable, and I have no idea what to think. But I do know that if she tries to tell me last night was a mistake, it will crush me.

Rather than meet my eyes, Natalie turns toward the kitchen and sets her purse on the counter.

"I tried to call you earlier," I say. "I tracked down Jack at the bar."

"Yeah. Sorry about that. I saw that I had missed you." She still hasn't looked directly at me; it's like she wants to do anything but be here in this moment having this conversation with me. Turning to the fridge, she fetches a bottle of water and takes a long sip.

When she sets her water bottle on the counter, I cross the room to stand before her and take her shoulders in my hands.

"Look at me, Nat." My voice is strained, barely above a whisper.

Finally, her blue eyes lift to mine, and *fuck me*. There's so much emotion reflected back at me that it makes me light-headed.

"Have you been crying?" I ask.

She gives me a small nod.

Shit. This is the last thing I wanted. "Why?"

I drop my hands from her shoulders, unsure if she wants me touching her, and instead clench my fists at my sides. I steel myself, waiting to hear that she regrets what happened between us, knowing it will crush me.

Her gaze drops from mine to the floor. "Talk to me, Nat. I spoke to Jack."

This gets her attention, and her eyes meet mine again. "What did he say?"

That's the moment I completely lose my nerve, because suddenly, I'm not ready to tell her I'm in love with her—not until I know if she thinks us hooking up was a one-time thing. "He . . . understood," I say instead. "He's not mad at us."

Her hand flies to her heart and her face relaxes. "Oh, thank God. I was freaking out all day, thinking I'd ruined everything."

I can't help but touch her again, taking her hands in mine. "You couldn't ruin anything. What happened last night, and at the hotel, that was on me. My fault. Completely."

Her lips curl up in a half smile. "I was a willing participant too, if you remember."

I smile back at her, meeting her eyes, and the tension in the room slides away for the first time since I arrived.

"You okay?" I ask, giving her hands a gentle squeeze.

"Yes . . . I think so, but what is this?"

"What do you want it to be?" I ask.

She thinks it over, chewing on her lower lip. "Is it crazy if I say I liked what we did last night?"

I chuckle and shake my head. "Not crazy at all, because I fucking loved it. I love you, Natalie. And not just as a friend." I know I'm about to lay all my cards on the table, but *fuck it*. "I'm not sure when it happened, but somewhere along the way, I fell in love with you. You're funny and smart and loyal and driven."

She smiles up at me, her gaze locked on mine.

"You suck at poker, and you can't bake to save

your life. But you're mine, and you have been since the moment I met you all those years ago."

Fresh tears are back in her eyes, only this time they're happy tears. She brings her arms around my neck and gives me a squeeze.

"Cam . . ." Her voice is hoarse with emotion.

"So, where were you all day?" I ask, suddenly curious about where she went and what she did after I left her in bed this morning.

She chews on her lower lip. "I needed time to think. I went back to our old spot at the lake. Then I drove around for a while. Stopped and had a doughnut."

I laugh, and Natalie smiles. "Come here." When I pull her to my chest, she doesn't resist, folding her body into my much taller frame. It feels so good just to hold her like this. I could stay like this forever.

"Cam?" she murmurs.

"Hmm?"

"What did Jack say?"

A smirk tugs at my lips as I remember our conversation this morning. "He said it was about time."

She pulls back, meeting my eyes with confusion.

I reach into my pocket and pull out my half of the heart-shaped pendant that matches Natalie's. "I guess he knew. Shit, I guess I knew a long time ago too, if I'm being honest with myself."

She reaches under her shirt and lifts out the delicate chain that holds her half of the pendant. "I wore it last night. You didn't notice."

I noticed, but I don't tell her this. "Guess I was just a little distracted by how good you looked in that orange dress."

"It was tangerine," she says softly.

"Whatever it was, I wanted it off of you."

"I can't believe you saved that other half all these years." She sounds truly astonished.

"Of course I did."

She really has no idea how deeply I feel about her.

"I've been in love with you since I was sixteen,

Natalie."

A single tear slips down her cheek, and I reach down to wipe it away with my thumb.

"It's okay if you don't feel the same way," I tell her.

She shakes her head. "You've always been an amazing friend, everything a girl could want, but these last few weeks . . . my feelings have turned into something more too. I love you, Cam."

Her words are everything. I tug her against me, probably with more force than necessary. But, fuck it, I've been patient for what feels like forever, and I'm done taking my time. My lips crash against hers in a hungry kiss, and Natalie lets out a soft whimper that obliterates the last of my self-control. Her lips part, and I deepen our kiss, my tongue licking against hers. I feel her hands tighten into my shirt as she claws her way closer.

My heart is near bursting with so much emotion, and now my cock has gone rock hard.

I lift her into my arms, and Natalie wraps her calves around my hips. I walk her over to the dining table. When I set her down, our lips only part long enough to pull off shirts over our heads, and push pants and underwear out of our way.

We're frantic with need, even though I was inside her twelve hours ago. Suddenly, I'm starved for her. And somehow, miraculously, it seems she feels the same.

"Cam," she moans.

"Yes, baby. Tell me what you need."

The head of my hard cock is pressed against her damp core, and she's grinding her hips all over me, getting me wet, and *fuuuck*, making me lose my mind.

I press one finger inside her snug channel while Natalie groans and grabs my ass.

"Need you," she murmurs against the crook of my neck.

"Let me get you ready first," I say.

She shakes her head, suddenly resolute. "No. Now. Please."

She's right. I can't wait any longer either. I've gotta give the lady what she wants. Aligning myself against her heat, I press forward. Apparently, neither of us can be bothered with a condom. I know Natalie's on birth control; half the time I'm the one who has to remind her to take it. And I'm certain we're both clean.

I intend to go slow, to ease into her and make her feel good, but that's not what happens. The feel of her bare is better than anything I've ever felt. Soon, I'm pumping my hips and gripping her curvy ass to bury myself deeper with each and every thrust.

"Fuck, Natalie," I say on a groan.

"Oh God, yes. Yes," she pants. "Right there. Don't stop."

I couldn't even if I wanted to.

It feels so good, so right, so perfect.

Then suddenly, I feel her shift in my arms and hear a loud creak.

The hell?

Natalie starts laughing, seeming to realize what happened before I do. "We broke the table."

"Shit. Sorry." I lift her into my arms and stalk toward her bedroom. It's a little difficult walking with my pants tangled around my ankles, and by the time I drop her onto the mattress, we're both laughing.

God, I never want this to change.

This. This right here is exactly how love is supposed to feel.

"This will be a little safer," I say.

She nods in agreement as I move over top of her. "In a bed. Yes. Now, come here."

I can't deny her, and when I thrust forward, we both release a long exhale.

Together, we move slower this time, and there's so much emotion reflected back at me when I gaze into her eyes, I almost lose it.

Then I lean down and bring my mouth to hers, and we kiss deeply, our first time as a couple.

CHAPTER
Twenty

Natalie

I couldn't be happier with my legs entwined with Cam's. His soft hair tickles my chin, and I breathe in his masculine scent. Somehow, we made it to the bed. I honestly can't remember much with my body humming like this. The details of our last sexual encounter are lost in the chemicals flooding my body. I don't mind, not one single bit. I'm certain we'll be making plenty more memories in the days, weeks, months, and years to come. After all, we have a decade's worth of sex to make up for.

Can I always feel like this?

Cam drops little kisses on my collarbone, and I shiver in delight.

Okay, maybe some details aren't lost to me.

"What's so funny?" he asks me, readjusting so we're at eye level.

"My boyfriend has a huge dick," I state matter-of-factly.

"I'm flattered." He laughs. "I like that word."

"Huge?"

"Well, yes." He chuckles, the sound rich and deep. "But more so *boyfriend*. I like the idea of being your boyfriend. I can't say I ever expected that."

I nuzzle into the crook of his neck, burying my smile in the silky-soft skin there. If I could hide away in this little pocket of comfort forever, I would in a heartbeat. I'd much rather stay here than think about any of the other bothersome things in life. Speaking of which . . . "You broke my table," I say, pouting. Cam wraps his arms tighter around me. My rib cage is flush against his. He's warm and firm and perfect against me.

"I'll buy you a new one," he promises, dropping yet another kiss on my forehead. I'll never grow tired of these small gestures of affection. They're just as powerful as any passionate embrace or intimate touch.

"I love that about you," I say. I run my fingers along the muscles in his back, earning me a sexy smile.

"Love what about me?"

"My money," I begin, and then correct myself. "My *family's* money. It's never mattered to you."

"Why would it?" Cam asks with furrowed brows.

"Ben always let me pay." I roll my eyes. The more time I spend with Cam, the more I realize what a douchebag Ben was, and how much time I wasted with other guys when the one I wanted was right in front of me the whole time.

"Okay, Ben was an idiot, plain and simple." Cam traces a line down my body, from shoulder to hip. "And let's never talk about your ex-boyfriend while you're naked."

"Oh, I'm so sorry," I whisper. "What would you rather talk about while I'm naked?"

"Well . . ." His eyes darken, lustful. "I'd like to

talk about how you get goose bumps every time I touch you. Even the slightest . . ."

I gasp as his fingers dance across my lower abdomen. I don't mind where this little game is headed. "Oh yeah? What else?"

"I'd like to talk about how soft your skin is," he murmurs into my chest as he trails soft, featherlight kisses down my sternum. His hands find my hips, keeping me tight against him.

No need. I'm not going anywhere.

"How badly I've wanted to touch you . . . just like this." Cam draws a small circle with the tip of his nose around my breast. I hold my breath as he licks a line to my nipple. Then I moan.

"And the sounds you make when I do that." I can feel his smirk against my skin.

"What else?" I breathe, already dizzy with lust.

"And the way that you move against me . . ."

His voice disappears into the plateau of my abdomen, where he plants hard, pulling kisses. I lean into it, especially as the touches journey lower and lower.

"The way you taste . . ."

My fingers tangle in his messy hair as he dips between my legs.

Oh shit.

This conversation is over. We're moving on to more interesting matters. I close my eyes and melt into him. With each caress of his lips and tongue, I can feel how much he loves me.

And with each shuddering breath I take, I can feel just how much I love him.

CHAPTER
Twenty-one

Natalie

"Be good, kids," Jack teases, setting two beers in front of us on the bar top.

I roll my eyes. "We're always good."

Cam smiles, bringing his bottle of beer to his lips.

I take a sip as Jack watches with an amused expression. "Just remember, dude," he says to Cam. "Just because you guys have been friends forever doesn't mean you're off the hook for wooing her."

I grin at this, sitting straighter on my bar stool. "Yes to wooing. I would like some of the woo."

Just imagining Cam releasing the full forces of

his charms my way sounds delightful. We've been dating seriously for a few weeks now, and so far he's been the perfect boyfriend. But that doesn't mean I can't tease him right along with Jack.

We've been on dates to the movies, to dinner at my parents' house, to the Mexican restaurant I love, and my favorite of all—the day I met him for lunch at the hospital and got to see my hot doctor boyfriend dressed in scrubs and interacting with a little patient. I think I fell even more in love with him that day.

Cam excuses himself to go to the restroom, and Jack leans over the bar toward me. "Just so you know, if he hurts you, I've vowed to skin him alive."

I grin at him. "Works for me."

When Cam returns, Jack stops wiping down the bar to chat with us for a minute longer. "Where are you two crazy kids off to tonight?"

"It's a surprise," Cam says, smiling at me.

I squint at him, wondering what he has in mind. Normally, we grab a casual dinner together and then head back to one of our places to hang out.

And it's usually mine since there's no chance of a roommate interrupting us.

Jack scurries off to help a group of ladies who are obviously here for a bachelorette party.

"You want to head out?" I ask once our drinks are mostly empty.

Cam smirks. "You eager to see what I have planned?"

"I've got to see if you're finally getting the hang of this whole boyfriend thing," I tease.

"I'm an amazing boyfriend," he says defensively, helping me out of my seat.

I merely pat his cute butt in encouragement as we head out into the parking lot. Soon Cam is settled into the driver's seat of his car, and I'm tucked in beside him.

"Where are you taking me?" I ask. We've turned onto a picturesque side street in a quaint little neighborhood just outside the city. "I've always loved this neighborhood, but there's nothing here but houses. All the restaurants are two blocks over."

"I know," he says, still smiling.

The car slows to a stop in front of a white two-story house with black shutters and planter boxes beneath the windows that I imagine look beautiful bursting with flowers in the spring. There's a FOR SALE sign in the front yard.

Butterflies dance in my stomach. "Cam? What's this?"

He puts the car into park and turns in his seat to face me, lifting my hand into his lap. "I can't live with Jack forever. We'll need our own space."

"And this . . ." My hand flies to my mouth.

"I want to buy it for us. But only if that will make you happy. Come look?"

Tears fill my eyes as I nod. "It's beautiful. You crazy man." And then I'm out of the car and heading up the front stone walkway toward the most beautiful home I could have ever dreamed of.

Cam opens the door and says something about four bedrooms that we'll need to work on filling up, and I let out a little squeal of excitement. It's perfect.

As I wander the spacious rooms with this amazing man by my side, I wonder briefly if this is what it feels like when all your dreams come true.

Epilogue

Natalie

"Where am I supposed to stand?" Jack whispers in my ear.

I turn to him with wide eyes. We're hiding behind a lace partition separating us from the rest of the ceremony.

"What do you mean, where do you stand? Where did you stand during the rehearsal?"

"Shit, I don't know. I'm nervous. It's hard to be both maid of honor and best man, okay? Very disorienting."

"Oh, I'm so sorry that we inconvenienced you with our friendship," I say, rolling my eyes. It only made sense that our best friend should have every major role in the wedding, excluding the role of officiant. If he had been comfortable with it, I would have loved to have Jack perform the ceremony. That's where he drew the line.

"No way," he said when we pitched the idea. "Get a damn priest. I'm not about to be responsible for the legality of your union."

The wind ruffles the curtains, and I get a peek at the few guests at our ceremony. Cam's parents sit comfortably on his side of the aisle, along with Tyron, Max, and a few friends from work. My side consists of our female friends from college and my support squad of Mandy and Janelle. The bridal party is wearing a shade of green Cam and I have insisted is *sage.* It's far from glamorous, but it did make Cam and me laugh. If I had to wear pumpkin-tangerine in my last round as a bridesmaid, then my ladies can wear baby-puke green.

Meanwhile, my parents sit side by side, whispering anxiously to each other. They're probably wishing they could have spent a few extra thousand dollars on the location. Or at least that I had agreed to a longer guest list so they could have included all of their philanthropist friends.

But this is perfect. A destination wedding in

Hawaii with only our closest friends is more than either Cam or I could have dreamed of.

The curtains waft closed again.

"Are you nervous?"

"I don't know," I admit. "There are a lot of emotions."

"Yeah. I can't believe my two best friends are about to get married." Jack wraps me in his arms with a big, happy sigh.

"You better believe it," I whisper into his chest. I can barely believe it myself, yet it feels so right. So inevitable.

"You ready?" Jack holds out his phone, his finger hovering over it.

"Fuck yes."

With the tap of a finger, Jack starts the music. It's a simple, cheesy orchestral version of "Here Comes the Bride." I laugh and loop my arm through his. Together, we part the curtains.

My heart clenches when I see him.

Cam.

He's a pillar of confidence and strength, with a look on his face I want to remember for the rest of my life. We're so close to the shore that the small waves almost lap at his bare feet. My heart clenches. I take in all of him, from his cool linen pants to his fitted white button-up shirt, to that smile brighter than the sun shining down on us. I can feel my mother scoffing at his choice in casual clothes, my father sighing at his decision to not wear a tie.

But there he is, simply himself. Cam's hair whips this way and that in the wind. His cheeky grin makes my heart soar. I would run to him and jump in his arms if I weren't holding on to Jack so tightly.

"You look beautiful, by the way," Jack whispers in my ear. "In case it wasn't obvious."

I blush. My wedding dress is far from extravagant. It is a simple white gown with a sweeping neckline and trailing skirt. And it's comfortable, which means I can actually enjoy my evening without worrying about an over-frilly gown.

Keeping the dress a secret from Cam was one of the hardest things I've had to do in the course of our relationship. I'm so used to modeling my outfits for him, relying on his opinion to make my decision. This, however, was one outfit I didn't want his opinion on. Not until the very last moment.

And by the look on his face, it was worth it.

When Jack delivers me to his best friend's side, he wraps us both in a tight hug.

"Jack, I can't breathe," Cam wheezes. I would laugh if I weren't being smothered by his arms as well.

"Sorry," Jack says, releasing us. "I just had to do that. Go get married or whatever."

He steps aside, and all I can see is the man before me. Cam's eyes are filled with such emotion, such love, that it makes my breath catch. From friends to lovers, soon to be partners, he and I have come a long way.

All we can do is grin at each other like complete idiots.

"Wanna get married or whatever?" Cam whispers with a sly smile.

"More than anything."

• • •

The reception is held at our hotel resort. We're all tucked away under an outdoor canopy decorated with hundreds of tiny twinkling lights. The air is warm, fragrant, and full of laughter. There's plenty of wine and music and good company. The food has been nearly demolished. The cake, in particular, was Cam's idea. Instead of a classic tiered wedding cake, he thought a tower of doughnuts would be more up our alley. Juvenile? Maybe. Regrets? None.

Even my mother found Cam's choice of cake charming. She sits next to me now, holding my hand in hers. With wry smiles on our faces, we watch my new husband and Jack cut their best moves on the dance floor. We both laugh. This is a sweet and rare moment. I'm not going to take it for granted.

Unfortunately, our personalities always get in the way.

"It's silver?" my mother asks with a frown, and I realize she's inspecting my ring.

The ring is beautiful: a twisted, intricate band, tying me to my husband for better or for worse.

Cam and I decided to melt our half-heart pendants from forever ago into wedding rings, a symbol of our friendship transformed into our devotion to each other.

"Yes, we wanted silver," I say without explaining. I'd rather not get into the specifics with my mother. If I've learned anything, it's that she never quite understands my decisions. Besides, they are *our* rings. Our special connection. No one else needs to be privy to those details.

"Oh, honey. You know silver tarnishes, don't you?"

I could scream.

Really? Today? You have to be judgmental today?

Instead, I take a deep breath. "Everything tarnishes, Mother. Even a marriage. We'll polish it. Don't you think over the course of my years-long friendship with Cam that we've argued? That we've had our ups and downs? But we love each other and believe in this. Nothing can stay tarnished forever."

My mother is absolutely taken aback, staring at

me like I'm a stranger.

Or maybe she's finally seeing me for the first time.

Father appears at her side and rests his hand comfortably on her small shoulder. "They didn't have any pinot," he says, offering her a new glass of white wine. "I can't believe it. Next best thing."

My mother accepts the glass without breaking eye contact with me.

"What's going on here, ladies?" my father asks, ever the clueless one of the Moore household. "What did I miss?"

"Our daughter is just reminding me what it means to be in love," she says. Then, with a warm smile, she plants a soft kiss on my father's hand. He smiles back, kissing her on the top of her head.

I breathe a sigh of relief. I'm not convinced that my parents and I will ever learn how to exist in harmony.

But she listened.

It's a start.

Then my mother pulls me in for a one-armed

hug. "I know I don't tell you enough, but I'm very proud of you."

"Thanks, Mother." I smile at her.

"Care for a dance?"

Cam's voice is both a relief and an excitement. I turn to see my husband with his hand outstretched, beckoning me to join him.

My husband.

His own silver ring glitters in the low light.

"Take me away."

With a flourish, he leads me onto the dance floor. He pulls me in close, and I rest my head on his firm shoulder with closed eyes.

"First, I want to tell you how much I love your dress."

"Thank you. Second?"

His lips tickle the sensitive spot between my ear and my throat. "I can't wait to tear it off of you."

I grin at the low rumble of his words against my neck. "Hey now! I like this dress. And it has perfectly good buttons."

He brushes his hand down my back, the pads of his fingers bumping along the line of fasteners trailing down my spine.

"Perfectly good buttons are no buttons at all. Jesus, are there thirty of these?" He spins me to inspect, and I lean into him in my laughter. He kisses the back of my neck, wrapping his arms around me from behind.

"I love you." I sigh.

"I love you too."

It isn't until the guests have all trickled away to their respective hotel rooms that Cam and I get to be alone. Even Jack takes the cue to give us some space, stealing a bottle of red wine from the bar and sneaking away to find Meredith.

Within moments of saying good night to our parents and waiting for them to turn the corner, Cam has me pushed up against the door frame of our reserved suite. He places his knee between my legs, kissing me urgently on the mouth. I wrap my arms around the back of his neck, pulling myself up into his kiss as tightly as I can. A moment too soon, he breaks the kiss, his gaze searching my face.

What is he looking for?

"Natalie. My wife." His words are almost a question, like it's not real.

It is real.

"Say it again."

He kisses my eyelids, my cheeks, my nose. "My wife."

"Again."

In one sweeping motion, he scoops me into his arms and off my feet.

I kiss him softly on the lips. "My husband."

He opens the door and carries me over the threshold. The room takes my breath away. I squirm out of his arms and run toward the window. The view is spectacular, overlooking the waters sparkling under this evening's sunset.

He joins me, placing his own hand on top of mine where it rests on the glass.

"Shit," I mutter.

"What?" I can hear the edge of concern in his voice, ready to soothe any ache.

"It's silly."

"Tell me."

"I didn't get a doughnut." It's true. I was too busy bouncing between conversations to grab myself a "slice." How disappointing.

"Well then, you're very lucky that I asked the staff to wrap one up for you. It's in the kitchenette."

"There's a kitchenette?"

"This is what you're impressed by?"

To answer his question, I kiss him hard on the mouth with enough momentum to send us both tumbling backward onto the plush bed.

And we don't leave it for a very, very long time.

• • •

Thank you for reading about Natalie and Camden in Flirting with Forever!

Continue the story in *Dear Jane* and read all about Weston Chase, the sexy football player, and Jane, the one who got away. If you liked *Flirting with Forever*, you will LOVE *Dear Jane*!

.

Get a Free Book

Sign up for my newsletter and I'll automatically send you a free book.

www.kendallryanbooks.com/newsletter

What to Read Next

DEAR *Jane*

I broke her heart ten years ago and left town.

She hates me, and rightly so. It doesn't matter that the rest of the country loves me, that I'm a starting quarterback with a multimillion-dollar contract. Because when I look in the mirror, all I see is a failure who was too young—and too afraid—to fight for what I wanted.

But I'm not that guy anymore, and all I need is one shot to convince her.

• • •

He has no idea what happened after he left. And now I'm supposed to work alongside him like we don't have this huge, messy history?

But I'm older now, wiser, and I won't let anything stand in my way of doing a good job for this league. Not even one overpaid, arrogant player who thinks we're going to kiss and make up.

News flash, buddy: I am over you.

Get your copy at

www.kendallryanbooks.com/books/dear-jane

And read on for an exclusive sneak preview.

Sneak Peek of *Dear Jane*

CHAPTER
One

Jane

Nine times out of ten, when I tell people I work for a professional football team, they try to call my bluff. Usually, they make me repeat myself—"Come again?"—like they misheard me and I'm actually a manicurist or a dog sitter or something. Sometimes, they'll quiz me on players' jersey numbers or specific game plays, all of which I can answer without batting an eye.

I guess I can't blame people when they don't expect a pint-sized girl who loves heels and lipstick to be working in an industry of huge, muscular men pummeling each other into the turf for entertainment, but this world is all I know.

I was raised in a home where it was practically

law that I was on the couch to watch the Hawks game every Sunday afternoon, and my love affair with the sport hasn't stopped since. The fact that I get to work for the team I've been cheering for since I was in diapers seems almost too good to be true. Not to mention the fact that I have the most foolproof pickup line in any sports bar ever. Between traveling the country with the team and brushing shoulders with sports legends, football is my religion.

And then there are days like today. With all the paperwork falling off of my desk, you'd think a tornado hit the Chicago area and touched down only in my office. The season is starting in just over a week, and my to-do list is longer than the whole length of the field.

It doesn't help that Mr. Flores, the general manager of the Hawks, is offsite all day at a meeting, so as his executive assistant, I'll be picking up his slack. As if that weren't enough, there's a huge press conference tomorrow to get ready for. This day is going to require a refill on my coffee and a whole lot of gangster rap.

I slip in my earbuds and put on my best game face, envisioning the frozen margarita I'm going to order later as a reward. And then, just as I'm getting into the zone, there's a knock on my office door and in walks the head coach. Or as I like to call him, Dad.

"Hey, sweetheart, is it okay if I bother you for a second?"

Despite what a lot of people think, my dad didn't get me this job. He probably could have if I'd let him, but I've never wanted to use Dad's position to my advantage. I'm perfectly capable of paving my own way without being given a leg up. So I served my time selling tickets before I eventually worked my way up to having my own office.

"Sure, if it's important," I say, glancing at my watch. It feels rude not to make a little time for my own father, even if I am totally swamped today. Dad shuts the door behind him and plops down in the faux leather armchair across from my desk.

"I'd say it's pretty important," he says, dodging direct eye contact with me. "But you're not going to like it."

I survey my mountain of paperwork and give Dad my best "bring it on" smile. With everything on my plate today, I came in to work ready for battle. It would take something pretty catastrophic to throw me off my game.

"We're bringing on a new player."

My eyebrows perk up in interest. It's pretty unheard of to make changes to the roster this close to the start of the season. Plus, if the Hawks have been eyeing a potential new player, I should have been one of the first people to know.

"Really? Who?" I prop my chin in my hands, leaning in like a high school girl ready for the hot gossip.

Dad lets out a long breath, his lips tensing as he nervously adjusts his Hawks cap. "It's, uh . . . it's Weston Chase."

My stomach bottoms out. I must have misheard him. There's no way my dad just told me that Weston Chase—my first and only long-term boyfriend, the star of our school's football team who shattered my heart and touchdown-danced all over the pieces—is joining the Hawks.

"Excuse me?" I'll give him a chance to repeat himself and prove that I must be losing my hearing at an alarmingly young age. Please, *please* say another name. Any other name.

"Weston Chase. You remember him, right?"

"Are . . . are you k-kidding me?" I manage to sputter out as my whole body locks up. My heart literally stutters in my chest like it's threatening to stop.

This has to be a joke, some kind of preseason prank the guys on the team put him up to. Weston Chase is a thing of the past, a heartbreak nightmare I have left way, way behind me. What sort of terrible karma would bring him to the Hawks?

"I know it's not great," Dad says in what feels like the biggest understatement in history.

Rainy days aren't great. Fast food tacos aren't great. My ex-boyfriend stomping back into my life and turning my dream job into a nightmare? That's a fricking disaster.

Dad has no idea what really happened with Weston and me all those years ago. Almost no one knows. About the baby, about my heartbreak . . .

"I wanted to keep it under wraps in case it didn't end up happening," Dad explains, fiddling with the fraying edge of his hat. "I didn't want you getting all worked up for nothing. But Weston is meeting with the general manager today, so it looks like things are pretty set in stone. We're going to announce him as our new quarterback at tomorrow's press conference."

Tomorrow? So I have less than twenty-four hours to prepare to face the douchebag who shattered my heart into a million tiny pieces?

Just two minutes ago, I was ready for the day to fly by, eyeing my frozen margarita on the other side, and now I wish everything would just freeze for a second so I can stop my head from spinning. It's not like I didn't know Weston was a professional football player, no matter how hard I tried to block out any and all news about him since he was first drafted.

"Are you going to be all right, sweetie?" Dad asks.

I realize I haven't said anything as I stare into space. I've got to get a hold of myself.

"I don't really have a choice, do I?" I grumble through clenched teeth, rubbing my temples to ward off an impending stress headache.

"I'm sorry, sweetheart. I just figured it was best you heard it from me. I didn't want you bumping into the guy for the first time in almost ten years without a little fair warning."

Holy shit, almost ten years? Has it really been that long? Nearly a whole decade since I've seen Weston Chase.

It feels like just last week we were sneaking bottles of wine out of his parents' wine cellar and making toasts to his football scholarship in his backyard. That was the night before he left for college. We caught our first buzz off that wine, kissing and promising we'd talk on the phone every single day until he came home for Thanksgiving.

It seemed so perfect at the time. Now it just feels like a load of bullshit.

"Why the Hawks?" I ask, waving off that memory like the sour smell of a used jockstrap. "Can't he go play for literally any other team?"

"He *was* playing for another team. We're getting him from Philadelphia."

"And he couldn't have stayed there?" I snap, my sassy tone biting.

"Jane, let me get through the whole story, would you?"

I let my gaze fall apologetically to my desk, like a puppy who just got scolded. I shouldn't be taking my frustration out on Dad. The truth is, I'm glad he thought to come to me about this.

He's quiet for a second, drumming his fingers on the arm of his chair, probably trying to figure out the best way to go about it. When he speaks again, his tone is soft and careful, like he's treading through a minefield, worried I may explode at any second.

And I just might.

"You know our starting quarterback is out for the season with that ACL injury. Yeah, we have our backup, but you and I both know he's not good enough to carry us to the playoffs. And things weren't going great for Weston in Philadelphia. His fiancée cheated on him with their star linebacker. It was a real messy situation, Jane. He needed out of there, stat."

Is it bad that hearing that Weston got cheated on makes the corner of my mouth threaten a smile? I try to keep my best poker face, act like I'm not secretly pleased that Weston Chase got what was coming to him, but Dad immediately notices the snicker I'm holding back.

"Look, I don't know exactly what went down between you two," Dad confesses, putting his hands out in front of him in surrender, "and I don't want to know. Some things a father just doesn't need to know about. But I know you walked away with a pretty bruised-up heart."

More like limped away, or maybe crawled. Dad is making it sound like Weston and I ended on polite terms, like I made a full recovery after a few pints of brownie ice cream and a good cry or two. I wish it were that simple.

"It was . . . complicated," I admit, my throat going tight. I squeeze my eyes shut, pulling myself together the best I can. One way or another, I'm going to have to get through this. After a deep breath, I add, "But it was a long time ago."

Dad gives me his signature half smile that I know means he's proud of me. "You've got this, kiddo. And besides, this really is the best place for Weston. Back close to home, close to his mom and all. Plus, our backup kicker, Colin, is an old college buddy of his. He's the one who gave us the lead on recruiting Weston to the Hawks. I guess they used to live together, and he—"

I hold up a hand in protest, cutting Dad off from sharing any more details of Weston's life. If I'm going to be professional with him, I've got to stay far, far away from any of the personal stuff. "Need-to-know basis, Dad."

He gives me one firm nod. "Understood." He drums his fingers one last time on the chair and I glance at my watch again, silently ushering him out the door and ending this father-daughter moment.

"Well, I guess I'll leave you to scale your mountain of paperwork," he teases, gesturing to the chaos that is my desk.

I mentally thank my busy schedule for providing me with a good distraction from this Weston stuff.

"Thanks, Dad. Love you," I say, wiggling one hand in a wave as the other reaches for my to-do list.

Just as Dad twists the doorknob, he pivots and adds one final thought. "This might turn out to be a good thing, sweetheart. You never know."

I fake an enthusiastic smile, then grab a pen and scrawl one final item onto my to-do list.

Stay far, far away from Weston Chase.

• • •

One of the best things about being the executive assistant to the Hawks' general manager is that the spotlight is never on me. I have no interest in being the center of attention, so I'm happy to slip out of the shot when the cameras flash on Mr. Flores. And with the announcement of our last-minute roster addition, every reporter, blogger, and talk-show host in the country is clamoring to get a quote from him. Probably for the best that no one cares to hear my opinion on the matter, because I'd have a few choice words on our new player if any news outlet gave me the mic.

After our usual pre-press-conference routine of running a few practice questions in his office, Mr. Flores pulls two ties out of his lower desk drawer, holding each one up to his chest so I can get the full image.

"I know I'm being ridiculous," he admits. "But

you know that place is going to be packed with every major news outlet."

I smirk, pointing to the navy tie in Flores's right hand. I'm glad I'm not the only one dressing to impress today.

I've got on my personal brand of battle gear—high-rise black skinny jeans with an army-green blazer, dark red lipstick, and the sexiest underwear I own. Not that anyone is going to see this little lacy black number, but just knowing I have it on is a major confidence boost.

And this press conference is going to take every ounce of confidence I can dredge up. I have half a mind to throw on a football helmet too, so maybe I can get through this press conference without Weston noticing or recognizing me, but I know I can't hide from him forever. If I don't face him now, I'll just have to do it tomorrow or the next day. No use putting it off.

And the last thing I want him thinking is that I'm cowering in the corner, fearful of him.

Mr. Flores gets one last look at himself in the reflection of his window, smoothing out his suit jacket and giving himself a nod of approval.

"Ready?" he asks, tightening the knot of his tie.

"As I'll ever be."

I follow Mr. Flores down the hall to the elevator, which takes us straight to the media room. As soon as the elevator doors slide open, the familiar flash of cameras greets us. I recognize all the usual photographers, but see at least a dozen unfamiliar faces. I guess bringing on Weston really is a big deal. A fifty-million-dollar big deal, if the rumors are true.

As Mr. Flores heads to the table to take his seat next to my dad, I slip to the back of the room. There's one empty chair onstage, but I know it won't stay empty for long. As if on cue, the locker-room door swings open and in comes my own personal blast from the past.

It pains me to say it, but Weston Chase looks damn good. Tall. Insanely fit. Cocky swagger.

But this isn't the high school heartthrob I fell for anymore. Ten years of weightlifting and endurance training have done him quite a few favors. He still has the same short brown hair, which is styled with gel, and his tight smile is as familiar as ever. All the things I loved about him haven't changed, and I'm sure that means all the things I've hated are the same too.

I inhale sharply and watch as he stalks toward his spot between my father and Mr. Flores. He holds up one hand to greet the crowd before taking his seat. Dad gives him a friendly slap on one broad, sculpted shoulder, which makes me twitch a little. It feels like a high school football game all over again with Weston in his jersey and me in the crowd.

And then it happens. He sees me. I should have blended in with the reporters, or at least kept from staring at him for so long, but it's too late. He spotted me, and he's not looking away.

Shit. Fixing my focus on Dad, I force myself to do my best impression of someone who gives zero fucks about his presence in this room, nodding along with my dad's answers as if I'm catching more than every third word. I sure as hell can't focus with Weston Chase's stare burning a hole in my cheek.

Even as the press turns their attention to Weston, I never once feel his eyes drift away from me. He answers in that same low, maple-syrup voice that

I used to love. That same deep voice that used to whisper against my neck how beautiful I was, how good I felt. It makes every hair on my body stand at attention.

Don't. You. Dare. Look. At. Him.

I force another breath into my oxygen-deprived lungs, and try not to act like my whole world wasn't just shaken.

What I'm sure is a twenty-minute press conference feels like a century, but things finally come to a close. As the room clears out, Weston disappears into the locker room in the blink of an eye. Finally.

I take a much-needed pull of oxygen. I did it. I survived.

"Jane! Over here!"

I scan the room for the source of the request— it's Mr. Flores. He waves me over as he chats one-on-one with a perky blond reporter.

"Jane, can you do me a huge favor? This woman from the *Times* wants to chat with Colin Crosley, number forty-one. He was Weston's roommate in college, and she's looking for a quote. Could you pull him out of the locker room for me?"

I gulp down the enormous lump in my throat. The locker room? You mean the place Weston *just* walked into?

I rack my brain for any excuse not to go in there, but I've got nothing that Flores would buy. He sends me in there to give messages to the players at least once a week. As the coach's daughter, I'm practically a sister to those guys, and half of them have underwear sponsorships anyway, so all of America has seen them almost naked. It's never been a big deal.

Until now.

"I've got it," I manage to say through a forced smile.

I square my shoulders, preparing myself for whatever I'm about to walk into. Just get in there, be professional, and get out. Nothing you can't handle. Maybe you won't even run into *he who shall not be named*.

I push open the heavy steel door and wander through the short hallway to the locker-room door. The double doors mean that no one can accidentally steal a peek of a player indisposed, but they also mean you can't see who's coming around the corner.

I must have pushed a little too hard on the locker-room door, because it swings all the way open, thwacking a nearby player. "Oops, sorry!"

And by a nearby player, I mean Weston Chase. And by Weston Chase, I mean Weston Chase wearing nothing but a pair of athletic shorts slung low on his trim hips. Just my luck.

I can't stop my mouth from falling open a little. I thought he looked good up there in his jersey, but that was nothing compared to the Greek god standing in front of me.

My gaze wanders from his broad shoulders to his smooth, defined pecs and perfectly carved abs. It's like all the air's been sucked from the room, and I can't even speak. Definitely can't raise my head and look at his eyes. I don't want to know what I'd find there. Amusement maybe? Curiosity about me, about the woman I've grown into? Or worse, indifference?

I swivel on the heels of my leather pumps, desperately looking for someone else, anyone else, I can talk to.

"What's up, Jane?" It's Alex, our best linebacker, one of my closest friends on the team.

Thank God.

"Hi, Alex." I sigh, my voice dripping with relief. "Could you send Colin out? The press wants a quote from him about . . ." I swallow the rest of the sentence, clenching my hands into fists to keep them from shaking.

Alex looks around the locker room, scratching at the scruff on his cheek. "Weston, have you seen Colin?"

Really, Alex? Really? Give me a fricking break. I don't dare stick around to catch Weston's response. I've got to get out of here.

"Just find him and send him out ASAP," I rattle off in my sternest assistant-to-the-manager voice.

Alex shoots me a concerned look, his eyebrows knitting together. "You okay, Jane?"

I don't bother answering, too worried that I might tell the truth. Instead, I push the locker-room door back open and strut out with whatever pride I have remaining.

One press conference down, an entire season to go.

Find out more and get your copy at

www.kendallryanbooks.com/books/dear-jane

Acknowledgments

Thank you so very much to my wonderful readers! You make all of this possible, and even though some days are stressful, I don't take a single minute of that for granted.

I'm so grateful to my amazing team . . . you guys are incredible. Pam Berehulke, Alyssa Garcia, Danielle Sanchez, Flavia Viotti, Becca Mysoor, Anthony Colletti, and Elaine York. I hate the thought of forgetting someone, but man, it takes a village, and I'm so glad you guys are part of mine.

Big squeezes to my husband, John, for the unending support he provides. I would thank my children, but let's be honest, they're four years old, and it's a wonder my books get written at all.

Biggest praise of all—thank you, God, for blessing me so richly, for letting me share my God-given talent of storytelling with the world and providing me with such opportunity. I pray that each and every one of my readers will find his or her own happily-ever-after.

Follow Kendall

BookBub has a feature where you can follow me and get an alert when I release a book or put a title on sale. Sign up here to stay in the loop:

www.bookbub.com/authors/kendall-ryan

Website

www.kendallryanbooks.com

Facebook

www.facebook.com/kendallryanbooks

Twitter

www.twitter.com/kendallryan1

Instagram

www.instagram.com/kendallryan1

Newsletter

www.kendallryanbooks.com/newsletter

About the Author

A *New York Times*, *Wall Street Journal*, and *USA TODAY* bestselling author of more than two dozen titles, Kendall Ryan has sold over two million books, and her books have been translated into several languages in countries around the world. Her books have also appeared on the *New York Times* and *USA TODAY* bestseller list more than three dozen times. Kendall has been featured in publications such as *USA TODAY*, *Newsweek*, and *In Touch Magazine*. She lives in Texas with her husband and two sons.

To be notified of new releases or sales, join Kendall's private Mailing List.

www.kendallryanbooks.com/newsletter

Get even more of the inside scoop when you join Kendall's private Facebook group, Kendall's Kinky Cuties:

www.facebook.com/groups/kendallskinkycuties

Other Books by Kendall Ryan

Unravel Me

Make Me Yours

Working It

Craving Him

All or Nothing

When I Break Series

Filthy Beautiful Lies Series

The Gentleman Mentor

Sinfully Mine

Bait & Switch

Slow & Steady

The Room Mate

The Play Mate

The House Mate

The Bed Mate

The Soul Mate

Hard to Love

For a complete list of Kendall's books, visit:

www.kendallryanbooks.com/all-books

WITHDRAWN

CPSIA information can be obtained
at www.ICGtesting.com
Printed in the USA
LVHW031432231218
601536LV00004B/404/P